# The WEDDING

A story of hope, music, and redemption

From the Beloved Christmas Bell Ringer Series

I0570888

# Copyright Page

# Fiction Disclaimer (Fiction Statement)

## Table of Contents

# Introduction

Welcome back to Pineville.

If you have traveled with us through The Christmas Bell Ringer, you have already met Jack, Emily, Sue, and Tyler a group whose lives were intertwined with faith, music, and second chances. You witnessed Jack's return to his hometown, the rekindling of old friendships, and the redemption of a young man named Tyler who found guidance and hope through Jack's quiet mentorship.

In The Wedding, the story continues. Jack and Emily's relationship moves toward a joyous celebration, but they are not the only ones discovering new beginnings. Tyler and Sue, once just friends navigating the chaos of the Christmas concert season, find their own bond deepening in unexpected ways. Their blossoming relationship adds a new layer of warmth and discovery to the tapestry of Pineville's close-knit community.

As Jack and Emily prepare for their wedding facing snowstorms, last-minute changes, and the ever-present charm of their small-town lift Tyler and Sue are learning to navigate the first steps of young love. Their connection reminds us of all that love does not wait for perfect timing; it grows in moments shared, laughter exchanged, and quiet, supportive glances when the world feels uncertain.

Whether you are returning to Pineville after The Christmas Bell Ringer or discovering this sequel for the first time, you will find a story that weaves together faith, family, and the courage to start anew.

So, settle in, and let The Wedding unfold its gentle tale of love in all its forms from a wedding altar to a diner booth, from a record store to a church pew where every relationship is a testament to the grace of God and the beauty of second chances.

# Chapter One: Christmas Day

The scent of glazed ham filled the air as Jack Whitaker stood at the kitchen counter, carefully carving slices for their Christmas meal. A soft hum of conversation and laughter floated in from the living room, where Emily was chatting with Sue, her friend and record store assistant. Tyler sat cross-legged on the floor near the crackling fireplace, teasing the family cat with a dangling ribbon of tinsel.

Jack could not help but smile. This was his first Christmas in Pineville in over a decade, and for the first time in years, he felt like he belonged. The warmth of the wood stove, the glow of the tree lights, and the simple presence of Emily and Tyler made his heart ache in the best possible way.

"Jack," Emily called from the living room, "how is the ham coming along? Sue and I are starving."

"Almost ready," he replied, arranging the caramelized slices on a serving platter. He turned to check the oven, where scalloped potatoes were bubbling and golden, the perfect complement to the sweet and savory ham.

Sue poked her head around the corner; her cheeks flushed with the glow of the firelight. "You are making me rethink my plans for Christmas dinner next year, Jack. This smells incredible."

Jack chuckled. "Do not get use to it. I am only showing off because it is my first Christmas back."

Emily appeared at his side, brushing her hand along his arm. "It is more than that, Jack. You are home."

Home. The word settled over him like a warm quilt. He looked at Emily, her blue eyes sparkling with gratitude and something deeper love. His gaze flickered to Tyler, who was now setting the table with mismatched plates and napkins, humming a Christmas tune under his breath.

For the first time in a long while, Jack realized he was not just back. He was part of something.

As they gathered around the table, Sue raised her glass of apple juice. "To Jack and Emily. To Christmas. And to new beginnings."

They clinked glasses, and Jack offered a quiet prayer of thanks. When he looked up, his gaze met Emily's across the candlelit table. They did not need words to know what the other was thinking.

This was just the beginning.

As they continued eating, the conversation meandered between funny stories and local gossip. Tyler was finishing a second helping of scalloped potatoes while Jack refilled Sue's glass of apple juice. The flicker of candlelight danced against the windows, and the snow outside fell steadily, softening the world beyond the cozy dining room.

Between bites of ham, Tyler looked up from his plate, his tone casual but his curiosity clear. "So... when's the big day?" he asked, glancing between Jack and Emily. "Have you folks thought about it? Are you going to get married before heading to Nashville?"

The question settled into the warm air like a gentle pause. Jack and Emily exchanged a quick glance. Emily reached across the table and laced her fingers with Jack's, her voice calm but resolute.

"We've been thinking about it," she said softly. "For us, it is important to start this new chapter of Jack's music, our family on the right foundation. Getting married before Nashville is not just about organization; it is about honoring God and the commitment we are making to Him and each other."

Jack nodded, his voice steady. "We want to build our life together in a way that reflects our faith. Marriage is not just a step it is a covenant. We would rather begin our journey as husband and wife, grounded in our beliefs, than wait until later."

Sue set down her fork and nodded thoughtfully. Tyler, though still young, seemed to understand the weight of their words. He looked between them, his expression serious but touched with pride.

Emily glanced at Sue and Tyler, her eyes hopeful. "Of course, we will need to see if you two are willing to stand with us Sue as my maid of honor, and Tyler as Jack's best man. And we will need to check your schedules. We want a date that works for both of you."

Tyler's face brightened, his grin stretching wide. "Seriously? You want me to be your best man?"

Jack chuckled, reaching over to lightly tap his shoulder. "Absolutely. You are family, Tyler. There is no one else I would rather have standing with me."

Sue dabbed at her eyes with a napkin, a soft smile on her face. "You can count me in. I would be honored to stand with you, Emily."

Emily beamed, gratitude shining in her eyes. "Thank you both. That means the world to us."

Jack lifted his glass. "To family. To faith. And to new beginnings."

They clinked glasses again, the sounds of laughter and conversation blending with the quiet crackle of the fire. Outside, the snow continued to fall, blanketing the world in white.

Inside, wrapped in the warmth of shared hope and love, Jack and Emily knew this was just the beginning.

As they continued eating and passing around the last of the bread, Emily rose to bring dessert a tray of homemade apple pie and a dish of whipped cream. Jack followed with plates and forks, setting them on the table as the conversation turned to lighter topics.

Sue leaned forward, inhaling the scent of cinnamon and baked apples. "Emily, this pie smells amazing. You have outdone yourself today."

Emily smiled, slicing generous portions and passing them around. "Thank you. It is a family recipe, and I thought today was the perfect time to share it."

As they each dug into their slices, Tyler licked his fork and leaned back in his chair. "You know, school starts back on January 4," he said between bites. "I don't think I have anything that would be in the way of a wedding before Nashville."

Jack raised his eyebrows, his eyes meeting Emily's. "That's good to know," he said, his tone thoughtful.

Sue set her fork down and glanced at Emily. "If you decide on a Saturday evening wedding, we will only have to close the store for a few hours. I can run it until noon, and then we can head to the church. It would not be a problem at all."

Emily's eyes shone with gratitude. "That is so thoughtful of you, Sue. Thank you. We will keep that in mind when we start looking at dates."

Jack nodded in agreement. "We just need to check the calendar and coordinate with everyone. We want a day that works for all of us."

Sue chuckled. "Well, we are all on the same page here. Let us make it happen."

Tyler grinned, finishing the last bite of his pie. "Best Christmas ever," he declared, glancing at Jack with a sense of pride.

Jack smiled, his hand reaching across the table to squeeze Emily's. "I couldn't agree more."

The warmth of the meal, the laughter, and the shared hope wrapped around them like the glow of the fire. Outside, the snow continued to fall, a gentle reminder that even in winter's chill, new beginnings were already stirring.

After dessert, as plates were cleared and coffee poured, Sue glanced at her watch. "It's getting late, but if we're serious about this wedding, maybe we should at least check with Pastor Raymin."

Emily hesitated. "On Christmas Day? I would hate to bother him."

Jack smiled softly. "It is just one quick call. And it will give us something solid to plan around."

After a moment's silence, Emily nodded and reached for her phone. She scrolled through her contacts and tapped the number, holding her breath as it rang.

"Hello?" The pastor's voice came through, warm but a little groggy.

"Pastor Raymin, it's Emily," she said quickly. "I am so sorry to call you on Christmas Day. We were just talking over dinner, and we wanted to check your availability in January."

There was a soft chuckle on the other end. "Emily, no need to apologize. It is Christmas, and I am always happy to hear from my church family. What date were you thinking?"

Emily glanced at Jack, who leaned forward. "January 16, if that's possible," he said into the phone. "That would give us time to get everything ready, and then Emily and I can fly to Nashville on the 18th to record the album."

There was a brief pause before Pastor Raymin replied. "That works perfectly. Let us set it for January 16. I will mark it on my calendar right now. And congratulations, both of you. I am honored to be a part of this."

Relief and gratitude flooded through the room. Emily smiled as she ended the call. "He is on board for January 16. That gives us three weeks to plan."

Sue clapped her hands. "Well, I will make sure the store is covered that day. We will make it happen."

Tyler grinned. "And I'll make sure my schedule is clear though I'm pretty sure I wasn't going to be busy anyway."

Jack laughed softly, reaching for Emily's hand. "Then it is settled. January 16."

The group exchanged warm smiles, the quiet joy of the moment settling around them like the snow outside. In that simple, unplanned conversation, Jack and Emily's future had taken its first real shape a wedding, a journey to Nashville, and a new beginning they would face together.

# Chapter Two: Three Weeks to Plan

The candles flickered low as the evening wore on, the last crumbs of pie and mugs of coffee lingering on the table. Tyler and Sue chatted quietly near the fire, while Jack leaned back in his chair, his gaze drifting to Emily.

He reached for her hand, his thumb brushing gently over her knuckles. "So," he said softly, "what kind of wedding would you like? Formal or informal?"

Emily hesitated, her gaze dropping to their intertwined fingers. "Honestly," she said, her voice low but steady, "I have never had a wedding. I would love something formal if we can pull it off in three weeks."

Jack smiled, warmth and admiration filling his eyes. "If anyone can make that happen, it's you," he said.

Sue, overhearing, turned and added, "And you know we will all pitch in. I can help with decorations and anything else you need. We will make sure it is beautiful."

Tyler grinned from his spot by the fire. "I will help too. Whatever you need."

As Jack looked at Tyler, a realization struck him Tyler was just a teenager, without enough money for a tuxedo or wedding expenses. He glanced at Sue, remembering that she worked hard to keep her small apartment afloat. He felt a quiet responsibility settle over him.

"I just want you both to know," Jack said, his voice firm but gentle, "that I have still got money from my last royalty check. I will cover the dresses and tuxedos. I do not want either of you to worry about the cost. This is our celebration, and I want you both to be part of it without any stress."

Sue's eyes widened in surprise, her hand resting over her heart. "Jack, that is so generous. You really do not have to"

"I want to," he interrupted softly. "You've both been there for us. It would not feel right with you standing beside us, and not have everything you need, without breaking your bank."

Tyler's cheeks flushed, and he ducked his head shyly. "Thanks, Jack. That means a lot."

Emily's eyes shimmered with gratitude. "Thank you," she whispered, squeezing Jack's hand.

The fire crackled softly in the background, casting a warm glow over the room. Jack met Emily's gaze again, his voice filled with quiet conviction. "So, a formal wedding it is. We will make it happen in three weeks."

They sat in comfortable silence, each of them envisioning what lay ahead a wedding filled with love, faith, and the promise of new beginnings.

The fire crackled softly as the evening wound down, the warmth of the day settling into a comfortable calm. Emily glanced at the clock, then reached for her phone. "I wonder if the bridal shop will be open tomorrow," she mused aloud. "Sue, do you think you'd be able to come with me to look at dresses?"

Sue grinned, pulling out her own phone to check. "I am sure they will be open. It is the day after Christmas, and they will want to catch the post-holiday rush. Let us plan on it. I will clear my morning, and we can head out early."

Jack leaned back in his chair, a playful smirk tugging at the corner of his mouth. "Now remember," he teased, "that royalty check won't last forever so no dress over ten dollars, okay?"

The room burst into laughter, Tyler nearly snorting his drink, and Sue chuckling so hard she had to dab at her eyes with her napkin.

Emily grinned and rolled her eyes. "I'll do my best to stay under budget," she teased back, her heart warmed by the moment.

Jack looked Emily in the eyes, "Em, this is a once in a lifetime event, I want this to be the best it can be for you!"

Tears rolled down Emily's eyes, "I love you so much Jack Whittaker!"

They kissed and Jack wiped away Emily's tears with his fingers.

Tyler said, "can we knock off the mushy stuff?"

As the laughter subsided, Jack turned to Tyler. "How about I pick you up Saturday morning, and we'll head into town to look for tuxedos?"

Tyler's eyes brightened. "That sounds great. I have never been fitted for one before."

Sue, thoughtful, tapped her finger on the table. "You know, peach-colored roses are available in January. We could use that as the accent color. It would be perfect for the season."

Emily nodded, her face lighting up. "I love that idea. Peach is soft and warm it is perfect for winter without being too bright."

Jack grinned, raising his glass once more. "Then it is settled. The guys will wear peach shirts with their tuxedo, and we will make it a day to remember."

They clinked glasses, the simple joy of the moment filling the room. As the snow continued to fall outside, their plans for the wedding and for their future together took shape, one shared laugh and thoughtful decision at a time.

As the evening wound down and the last mugs of coffee were set aside, Sue, and Tyler began to gather their things and say their goodnights. The snow had thickened outside, soft flakes drifting down like powdered sugar over the quiet street.

Tyler, ever the jokester, grinned mischievously as he zipped up his coat. "So, Jack," he said, his voice teasing, "now that you two are engaged, are you going to share Emily's bed tonight?"

Both Jack and Emily spoke at the same time, their voices firm and united. "No!"

Emily laughed, shaking her head as she glanced at Jack. "Jack has been a true Christian gentleman. He's stayed in his bedroom at night, and it would not be right for us to sleep together before we are married. We believe in honoring God in our relationship."

Jack nodded, a quiet smile on his face. "We kiss and hug, and sometimes we cuddle on the couch watching TV with the fireplace on, but when it is time for bed, we go our separate ways. It is not always easy, but it's the right thing to do."

Tyler's grin softened into a look of understanding and respect. "That's cool. I was just messing around."

Sue gave a soft chuckle, pulling on her gloves. "You two are setting a wonderful example. And it will make the wedding day more special."

Jack gave Emily's hand a gentle squeeze, his eyes shining with warmth and conviction. "That's what we're hoping for."

With final goodnights, merry Christmases and a few more shared smiles, Sue and Tyler stepped out into the snowy night, leaving Jack and Emily alone by the fire's glow. They stood for a moment, listening to the quiet crackle of the wood, the peace of the season wrapping around them like a familiar embrace.

Emily looked up at Jack and whispered, "I'm so glad we're doing this the right way."

Jack smiled, pulling her into a gentle hug. "Me too."

And as they settled into the couch for a little while longer, watching the fire flicker and the snow fall beyond the window, they knew their love was built on something deeper than fleeting passion it was grounded in faith, respect, and the quiet certainty of a shared future.

# Chapter Three: Closed Signs and Lunch Plans

Saturday morning dawned bright and clear, the snow from the past few days sparkling under the winter sun. Emily had gone to Sues house early to pick her up. They sat in the kitchen sipping coffee and bundling into coats as they prepared for their bridal shop adventure. Emily's heart was light with anticipation. The thought of finding her perfect wedding dress something she had dreamed of but never thought possible sent a flutter of excitement through her.

"I still can't believe we're doing this," she said as they drove through the quiet streets toward Brook Stone the next town over and bigger than Pineville with more stores...

Sue grinned, adjusting the scarf around her neck. "You deserve it, Emily. After everything you have been through, this is your time. We will find you the perfect dress, and you will be a stunning bride."

Emily smiled, her fingers tapping nervously on the steering wheel. "I just hope we find something that fits both the vision and the budget."

Sue laughed softly. "I will make sure you do not go overboard and keep the price under $10. They both laughed hard, remembering what Jack said jokingly earlier!

They both carried on more conversation and chuckled, their breath fogging the windows as they turned into the small shopping district. But as they approached the bridal shop, Emily's heart sank.

A handwritten sign taped to the door read:

Closed for extended Christmas break. Will reopen Monday.

Sue let out a low groan. "Seriously? After all this planning?"

Emily's shoulders slumped, disappointment washing over her. "I was really hoping to get this done today. Now we will have to wait until Monday."

Sue patted her arm reassuringly. "It is not the end of the world. Let us think of it as more time to plan. We will come back Monday if they can fit us in. After all its January we can pray they are not too busy."

Emily sighed, pulling out her phone to call Jack. She tapped his name and listened to the phone ring, hoping he was not facing the same problem.

Jack answered on the second ring, his voice warm but tinged with exasperation. "Hey, Em. Let me guess you are standing outside the bridal shop, and it is closed."

Emily let out a soft laugh, the sound mingling with the crisp air. "Exactly. A handwritten sign on the door. Extended break until Monday."

Jack chuckled on the other end. "Tuxedo shop has the same sign. Tyler and I drove over, and the place is locked up tight. Seems like everyone is taking a longer holiday, well you closed the record shop today for the same reason!"

Emily leaned against the car, her breath forming clouds as she spoke. "Well, I guess we'll have to put the shopping on hold. No sense stressing about it today."

"Agreed," Jack said, his tone warm and reassuring. "Why don't we all meet at the diner for lunch? We can regroup and make a new plan."

Emily glanced at Sue, who was nodding in agreement. "That sounds like an excellent idea. How about noon?"

"Perfect," Jack replied. "We'll see you there."

Emily ended the call, tucking her phone back into her coat pocket. She turned to Sue, her expression a mixture of resignation and determination. "Well, looks like we are all in the same boat. Let us head back and make the best of it."

Sue smiled. "And maybe order a slice of that amazing apple pie at the diner to cheer us up."

Across town, Jack slid his phone into his jacket pocket, shaking his head with a rueful smile. "Well, buddy," he said to Tyler, "looks like our shopping trip's a bust today. But at least we will get a satisfying meal out of it."

Tyler grinned, adjusting his coat. "I'm always up for the diner's burgers."

Jack laughed, ruffling Tyler's hair. "Let's head over there and make the best of it."

The streets were quiet as both pairs made their way to the familiar diner in Pineville. Inside, the air was warm and filled with the comforting scents of grilled food, coffee, and freshly baked pie. Emily and Sue arrived first, slipping into a corner booth by the window. Emily shrugged off her coat, feeling the tension of the morning begin to melt away.

Sue leaned forward, resting her chin on her hand. "Well, at least we tried. And who knows the extra days will give us time to come up with even better ideas."

Emily smiled. "You're right. I just... I was hoping to cross something off the list today."

A few minutes later, Jack and Tyler walked in, shaking the snow from their boots and waving as they spotted them. Jack's eyes lit up at the sight of Emily, and Tyler grinned as he slid into the booth beside Sue, gently pushing her against the wall as a joke!

"Tyler" Sue yelled. "Always the jokester just like Jack!"

Jack said, "I would never!" With a grin and a chuckle!

Jack said, pulling off his jacket and settling next to Emily. "It's not a bridal shop or tuxedo fitting, but at least we're together."

Emily leaned against him briefly, finding comfort in his presence. "That's all that matters," she murmured.

They ordered lunch burgers for Tyler and Jack, a chicken sandwich for Emily, and a salad for Sue. As they waited for their food, Jack glanced at Emily, his tone turning lighthearted. "Now remember, ladies, that royalty check will not last forever. So, no dress over ten dollars, okay?"

The group burst into laughter, Tyler nearly snorting his drink, and Sue wiping tears from her eyes.

Emily playfully swatted Jack's arm. "I'll do my best to stay within budget," she teased.

As the laughter faded, Sue tapped her fingers on the table thoughtfully. "You know, a peach-colored wedding sounds so wonderful the more I think about it! That will make a beautiful accent color for the wedding."

Emily's eyes lit up. "Peach is soft and warm it will work perfectly for winter."

Jack nodded. "And the guys can wear peach shirts with their tuxedo. That will tie it all together."

Tyler grinned. "I am cool with that. If I do not have to wear a bow tie."

Jack chuckled. "Deal."

Emily, "I agree Tyler" she said chuckling.

Their food arrived and Tyler offered grace, and as they shared a leisurely lunch, the earlier disappointments faded into the background. They laughed, planned, and imagined what the next few weeks would hold. Despite the setbacks, the day was a reminder that love, faith, and family were at the heart of everything they were building together.

And as the snow continued to fall outside, Jack, Emily, Sue, and Tyler knew that the journey to the altar though delayed by a few closed signs would be even more meaningful when they finally stood their side by side.

Jack leaned back slightly, his curiosity getting the better of him. "Sue, I've always wondered how you ended up working for Emily at the store?"

Sue set her fork down, her cheeks coloring lightly. "I started when I was sixteen. I was looking for a part-time job after school, and Emily was kind enough to give me a shot. Stocking shelves, running the register, you name it. Now I am twenty, and it feels like family there. I love it. Emily us like a second mom and best friend!"

Emily smiled warmly. "She has been a lifesaver, especially during busy seasons. And now she is practically running the place when I am not there. It will be great to know the store will run smoothly while we are in Nashville!"

Jack nodded approvingly. "That's clear. You have a good head on your shoulders, Sue. We are lucky to have you involved with the wedding plans too."

Sue grinned, though her cheeks flushed a bit more. "Thanks, Jack. I will do whatever I can to make it special for you and Emily."

As they dug into their food, the conversation shifted. Tyler, pushing a fry around his plate, spoke up. "You know, I always enjoy having my birthday during Christmas vacation. But the bad part is, Mom could not always afford a Christmas gift and a birthday gift. So, we would have cake on my birthday, December 28, and that was it."

Emily's eyes softened, and she reached across the table, covering Tyler's hand with hers. "Tyler, that is something we can change this year. How about we have a birthday party for you at the store after we close at three on Tuesday? You can invite your friends, and Sue can come too."

Sue's face brightened with genuine happiness. "I would love to! And I can bring cupcakes or whatever you want."

Tyler's face lit up. "Really? That would be awesome! And hopefully we will not get sick on your cupcakes!" He said jokingly!

Sue, gently slapped Tyler.

At that, Jack exchanged a teasing glance with Emily, a playful smirk tugging at his lips. "You know, Emily and I were just talking about how we should do something special for you, Tyler. A little surprise. But it looks like we will just have to plan it aloud now that Sue's coming too."

Emily giggled softly, her eyes twinkling with mischief. "Exactly. Besides, you two make a great pair you are both young, full of energy, and you get along so well. It is only natural we would want you both at the party. Right, Jack?"

Jack nodded, suppressing a chuckle. "Absolutely. Besides, someone must help you blow out all those candles, Tyler."

Tyler groaned, his face turning a shade of red that rivaled Sue's earlier blush. "You guys are ridiculous."

Sue laughed along, though a faint pinkness lingered in her cheeks. "Don't listen to them, Tyler. We're just friends."

Jack grinned, leaning back against the booth. "For now," he said, drawing out the words playfully.

Emily swatted his arm. "Behave, Jack," she said, though she couldn't hide her smile.

As the laughter died down, Sue glanced at Emily. "So, we're still on for peach-colored roses for the wedding?"

Emily nodded, her expression soft and certain. "Absolutely. Peach is perfect it is settled."

Jack chuckled. "And the guys will wear peach shirts with their tuxedo. It is all coming together."

They finished their meal amidst shared laughter and the warmth of family and friendship. Despite the closed shops and minor setbacks, the day felt lighter and more connected than any of them could have planned.

As they gathered their coats to leave, Jack gave Emily's hand a squeeze, whispering, "You know, even with a few hiccups, today turned out perfect."

Emily smiled, leaning into him. "That's because we're surrounded by the people we love."

And with that, they stepped out into the crisp winter air, hearts full and plans for both a wedding and a surprise birthday party forming in their minds.

They finished their meal amidst shared laughter and the warmth of family and friendship. Despite the closed shops and minor setbacks, the day felt lighter and more connected than any of them could have planned.

As they gathered their coats and prepared to leave, Jack glanced at the falling snow outside. "Looks like the roads are still decent," he commented, helping Emily into her coat.

Sue grabbed her scarf from the back of the booth, and Tyler was already pulling on his jacket, but as they were about to step through the door, Emily paused. A playful light danced in her eyes.

"Hey," she said, her voice rising just enough to get everyone's attention. "Let's not end the day so soon. How about we all go bowling?"

Jack froze mid-step, turning to look at her with a surprised smile. "Bowling? I have not bowled since I was a teenager over twenty years ago."

Sue perked up, her face lighting with a mix of nostalgia and excitement. "My eighteenth birthday party two years ago was a bowling party. It was so much fun!"

Tyler grinned, tugging his gloves tighter. "I am in. It sounds fun. I have only gone a few times, but I'm game."

Emily looked around at them all, her enthusiasm infectious. "I am no professional bowler either but come on it will be a blast! Besides," she said, with a sly grin aimed at Jack, "I insist you keep your royalty money for the wedding. This one's on me."

Jack laughed, a deep and genuine sound, shaking his head. "You're not giving me a choice, are you?"

"Not a chance," Emily replied, her smile widening. "Let's make some more memories today."

Sue laughed. "I'm in. I'll even keep score!"

Tyler grinned, rubbing his hands together. "And I'll try not to drop the ball."

Jack opened the diner door with a flourish, bowing slightly. "After you, birthday boy and bowling champ," he said to Tyler and Sue.

They stepped out into the crisp winter air, their breath fogging in the chill, as the idea of a spontaneous bowling outing lifted everyone's spirits. The earlier frustrations melted away as they piled into the cars, laughter echoing into the snowy afternoon.

As they headed to the local bowling alley, Emily glanced at Jack, her heart full. "See? Even the best-laid plans can turn into something better than we expected."

Jack smiled, his fingers brushing hers as he reached for her hand. "That is what I love about you. Always finding the joy in every little twist and turn."

And with that, they drove off into the wintry afternoon, ready to turn a day of disappointments into a night of strikes, spares, and laughter-filled memories.

The parking lot of the local bowling alley was dusted with fresh snow, but the warm glow of neon lights and the faint echo of pins crashing invited them inside. The familiar scent of rental shoes and oil on the lanes hit them as soon as they stepped through the doors.

At the front desk, a cheerful young clerk greeted them. Jack leaned against the counter and said, "Four pairs of shoes, please."

The clerk handed over the shoes, sizes checked and shuffled, and Sue added with a smile, "And can I get a score sheet for keeping track?"

The clerk chuckled, shaking his head. "Oh, we do not use those anymore. It is all computerized now. The screens above the lanes keep track for you."

They exchanged amused looks. "Well, I guess we're not going to get lost in the math then," Jack said with a laugh.

"And just so you know," the clerk added, "no practice balls. Your first roll counts as the first frame."

All four turned to him, groaning in unison, "No!"

Jack said, "maybe they should put the kids gutter guards up, so you don't get gutter balls!"

Sue yelled, "That's cheating Jack!" As they all laughed.

"This is going to be a low-scoring game," Emily muttered, and they all laughed as they laced up their shoes and headed to their assigned lane.

Emily giggled as she adjusted her borrowed shoes. "I'm no professional but come on it'll be fun!"

Jack grinned, testing the weight of a ball. "Just aim for the middle and hope for the best."

They set up for their first game, the screen lighting up with their names. The first few frames were filled with gutter balls, splits, and surprised cheers when a pin or two fell. Each roll was met with either groans or exaggerated applause, and no one seemed to care much about the score.

"Emily's up!" Jack called, clapping his hands. Emily lined up her shot, tongue peeking from the corner of her mouth, and rolled the ball down the lane with a hopeful twist. The ball wobbled, clipped the edge, and took down four pins. Everyone clapped and cheered.

"Hey, I'll take it!" she said, laughing as she turned back to them.

Jack's first roll went straight into the gutter. "Guess I'm a bit rusty," he admitted, grinning.

Tyler, with a confident stance, sent his ball smoothly down the lane, knocking down six pins. Sue was up next, and though her ball rolled slowly, it somehow clipped seven pins. Tyler and Sue exchanged a high-five, laughing at their surprising teamwork.

By the end of the first game, they crowded around the scoreboard as it tallied the scores: Emily with 120, Jack with 122, Tyler with 130, and Sue with 101.

Everyone burst into laughter, clapping Sue on the back. "At least you made it over a hundred!" Emily teased warmly.

"I'll take it!" Sue replied with a grin, tossing her hands in the air.

As the games continued, the atmosphere grew more relaxed and playful. The second game was filled with dramatic windups, playful trash talk, and exaggerated cheers for even the smallest victories. Sue and Tyler found themselves naturally pairing up, offering each other high-fives with every spare or strike they managed. Their shared excitement filled the alley with laughter.

In the third game, Sue lined up her shot carefully, rolling a slow but steady ball. It wobbled, then struck the pins exactly right, sending them clattering for a spare. Her eyes lit up as the screen updated with her success. Tyler, without thinking, rushed over to give her a quick, excited hug. Sue laughed, her cheeks flushing pink.

"Nice one, Sue!" Tyler said, grinning.

A few frames later, Tyler bowled a strike that sent his ball crashing into the pins with unexpected force. Sue, without hesitation, hugged him back, both laughing as Emily and Jack cheered from behind.

"I guess we're the bowling dream team," Sue teased, holding out her hand for a high-five.

"You bet we are," Tyler said, slapping her hand enthusiastically.

They played three games, filled with gutter balls, surprise spares, and the occasional strike. The scores stayed modest nothing above 150, but the fun was immeasurable. Each game ended with cheers, laughter, and playful ribbing, none of them caring much about the numbers on the screen.

As they slipped off their shoes and prepared to leave, Jack turned to Emily with a smile. "Well, that was a lot more fun than I expected, but I bet my back will feel it tonight using muscles I have not used in a long time!"

Emily leaned against him, her heart full. "It is not about how we score it is about the memories we make. I will give your back a massage if you need it!"

Sue, still flushed from the excitement, added, "I'm just glad I wasn't the only one with gutter balls tonight."

"And at least you made it over a hundred in the first game," Emily said with a wink.

They all laughed, gathering their belongings.

# Chapter Four: A Bold Ask and a Green Pickup

As they gathered their things from the lane, the laughter still echoing in the air, Emily tugged at Sue's sleeve. "Let's freshen up before we leave," she said with a smile. Sue nodded, and together they made their way toward the restroom, leaving Jack and Tyler by the benches, packing up shoes and jackets.

While the girls were gone, Tyler glanced at Jack, his hands fidgeting nervously. "Hey, Jack," he said, his voice dropping a notch. "Can I ask you something?"

Jack turned, curiosity piqued. "Sure, buddy. What's up?"

Tyler hesitated, then took a breath. "Would it be okay if I asked Sue out? For pizza and a movie... tonight? Since we're already out?"

Jack's grin spread wide. "Of course it's okay," he said, pulling out his wallet and handing Tyler enough cash for dinner and tickets. "Here this should cover it."

Tyler's face lit up. "Thanks, Jack!"

Jack reached into his pocket, pulling out the familiar green pickup key. "And if she says yes, take my truck for the night. Emily and I will ride home in Sue's car, and we will all meet back at Emily's house later to swap vehicles."

Tyler's eyes widened. "Really? You sure?"

Jack chuckled. "Just don't crash it and fill the tank before you bring it back."

A few minutes later, Sue and Emily returned from the restroom, still chatting. Tyler stepped aside with Sue, trying to sound casual but feeling his heart race a little. "Hey, Sue," he said, his voice warm.

Sue turned, her eyebrows raised in curiosity. "Yeah, Tyler?"

"I was wondering," he said, his confidence growing as he spoke, "would you like to go out for pizza and a movie... tonight? Since we are already out?"

Sue's cheeks flushed pink, and she smiled with a mix of surprise and happiness. "I'd love to!"

"Great!" Tyler grinned. "Jack said I can take his truck. We will just need Emily to take your car home."

Sue laughed softly. "No problem. I will let Emily know."

They rejoined the group, and Sue turned to Emily. "Emily, would you mind driving my car back to your place? Tyler's taking Jack's truck so we can go out for pizza and a movie tonight."

Emily's eyes sparkled with delighted surprise. "Of course, Sue! That works perfectly. We will all meet back at my house to swap cars later."

Jack and Emily exchanged a knowing glance, their subtle matchmaking success clear as they all bundled up and stepped into the crisp night air.

Laughter and lighthearted teasing filled the parking lot as Sue handed her keys to Emily.

"Just don't get any ideas about speeding, birthday boy," Jack teased, clapping Tyler on the back.

"Not a chance," Tyler grinned, holding the keys like a trophy.

As everyone climbed into their respective vehicles, they parted ways for the evening Tyler and Sue heading off for their impromptu date, and Jack and Emily driving home together in Sue's car, their hearts full of warmth and laughter.

The crisp winter air greeted them as they stepped out of the bowling alley, the snow beneath their boots crunching softly. Tyler, holding Jack's truck keys and feeling a mixture of nerves and excitement, glanced at Sue as they walked across the lot.

He hesitated for just a moment before reaching out his hand toward her. Sue, without missing a beat, slipped her hand into his, interlocking their fingers naturally. They both smiled, their steps slowing as they crossed the lot together.

Behind them, Jack and Emily paused mid-step, watching the two with warm smiles. "Look at them," Emily murmured softly.

Jack nodded, his voice low and full of quiet pride. "They would make a good couple. Sue's always been grounded, a solid Christian girl. And Tyler he is starting to find his way there too. They have us as examples."

Emily leaned into him, her breath forming soft clouds in the air. "They're sweet. It's nice to see something good growing between them. Tyler deserves that kind of friendship and more."

As Tyler reached Jack's green pickup, he turned to Sue and opened the passenger door with a slight flourish. "After you," he said, his tone playful but sincere.

Sue laughed softly, the sound light and genuine, and slid into the seat. As Tyler climbed in the drivers' seat, Emily and Jack exchanged another glance, noticing how Sue subtly shifted closer to Tyler in the seat, her shoulder brushing his just slightly.

Emily's heart softened, and she squeezed Jack's arm. "They're adorable," she said.

Jack chuckled, pulling Emily closer as they continued toward Sue's car. "Yeah, they are. They remind me of us just starting out, figuring it all out. But with a little help from above, they will find their way too."

As they each climbed into their respective vehicles, Jack and Emily could not help but smile as they watched Tyler and Sue pulling out of the lot, their laughter mingling with the glow of the dashboard lights. The green pickup's taillights disappeared into the falling snow, and with it, a sense of something new and hopeful taking root.

As Tyler and Sue pulled out of the lot in Jack's green pickup, Jack turned to Emily with a grin. "Well, looks like I will be playing chauffeur now," he joked.

Emily giggled, her cheeks flushed with the lingering warmth of the evening. "I don't mind one bit," she said.

Jack hurried around to the passenger side of Sue's car, pulling the door open with a playful flourish. "Your carriage awaits, m'lady," he teased.

Emily gave a dramatic curtsy before sliding into the passenger seat. "Thank you, kind sir," she said, her eyes twinkling.

Jack closed the door, rounded the front of the car, and climbed into the driver's seat. Just as he was settling in, he felt Emily's hand brush his arm and her shoulder shift closer. She slid over on the bench seat, nestling up against him, her breath warm against his cheek.

"This is fun," she murmured with a mischievous smile. "I haven't done this since high school... with, you know who."

Jack chuckled softly, though a flicker of memory passed through his mind. Emily did not need to say Chris's name. Jack knew. But instead of feeling threatened by old memories, he felt a quiet contentment settle over him. He was here now, with her, and they were building something new.

"I'll take that as a compliment," he said, giving her hand a squeeze.

Emily laughed softly, her head resting briefly against his shoulder. "It is. You have always been the better choice anyway."

They drove home through the softly falling snow, the streetlights casting a golden glow over the quiet roads. Once home, they kicked off their shoes, made simple sandwiches for supper, and settled onto the couch.

The flicker of a romantic movie on TV cast soft light across the room as they cuddled under a shared blanket, Emily's head resting against Jack's chest, his arm wrapped securely around her shoulders. The day's laughter and excitement had faded into a peaceful contentment, their hearts full of gratitude for simple moments shared.

As the credits rolled and the movie faded into a quiet hum, Jack pressed a gentle kiss to Emily's temple. "Best day we've had in a while," he murmured.

Emily smiled sleepily, nodding against him. "And it's just the beginning," she whispered.

Around ten o'clock, the familiar rumble of Jack's green pickup echoed down the street as Sue and Tyler pulled into his driveway. The headlights cut a swath through the snowy darkness before shutting off.

Sue parked the truck, glancing over at Tyler with a soft smile. "Thanks for tonight," she said, her voice warm.

Tyler grinned, his cheeks flushed from the cold and from the evening's fun. "Thank you. Best night I have had in a long time."

They sat in comfortable silence for a moment before Tyler said, "I guess I'll see you at church tomorrow?"

Sue nodded, her smile bright. "Definitely. I will pick you up around 10:30, if that's okay." She grinned and added playfully, "Unless you decide to drive Ole Betsy yourself. I mean, she's still the same old loud truck you've had since Jack passed her on to you."

Tyler laughed. "Yeah, Ole Betsy's running fine, but she is not exactly subtle. I think I will take you up on the ride. Gives us a little more time to hang out before church."

Sue's cheeks flushed a little deeper, and she nodded. "Sounds perfect. I will see you then."

Tyler gave a small wave as he climbed out of the truck and walked toward his house. Sue watched him go with a smile before shifting into gear and heading back toward Emily's to return Jack's truck.

When she arrived, she parked in the driveway and climbed out, Jack's green pickup keys in hand. Jack and Emily were already waiting on the porch, bundled up against the cold.

"How was it?" Emily called, her tone light and teasing as Sue approached. "Where's Tyler?"

Sue's cheeks colored slightly, but her smile was radiant. "It was great. Best impromptu date ever. Tyler suggested I drop him off to save me backtracking before heading home!"

Jack chuckled, exchanging a knowing glance with Emily. "Glad you two had fun. That's what it is all about."

Sue handed Jack his keys. "Here you go. Green pickup's running like a dream."

Emily handed Sue her own car keys in return. "Thanks for taking care of Tyler tonight. And Sue," she added with a gentle smile, "I expect to see you both in church tomorrow."

Sue grinned. "Wouldn't miss it. I will pick him up bright and early."

They shared a few more laughs and warm goodnights before Sue headed home, leaving Jack and Emily to enjoy the rest of their quiet evening. As the night settled in around them, a sense of peace and promise lingered in the air, setting the stage for a new day filled with faith, friendship, and the beginnings of something special.

# Chapter Five: A Special Announcement

Sunday morning dawned crisp and clear, the air carrying the promise of a new beginning. Jack and Emily arrived at the small country church early, bundled in coats against the lingering winter chill. The quiet hum of the furnace inside and the faint scent of old hymnals created a familiar comfort as they stepped into the sanctuary.

Pastor Raymin greeted them warmly, his handshake firm and his eyes kind. "Good morning, Jack, Emily," he said with a smile. "You're early today."

Jack nodded, glancing at Emily. "We wanted to talk with you before the service, Pastor. About the wedding."

Emily's cheeks flushed slightly, but her voice was steady. "With the wedding only a few weeks away, we would like to invite the whole congregation. There's just not enough time to send out formal invitations, and we would love for everyone to be part of it."

Pastor Raymin's smiles broadened. "That's a wonderful idea. I'll make the announcement during the service."

Relieved, Jack and Emily found seats in the front pew, their hearts light with anticipation. Moments later, the soft creak of the church doors heralded the arrival of Sue and Tyler. They walked in together, Tyler's face glowing with quiet pride, and Sue's with gentle warmth.

Tyler gave Jack a subtle nod as they approached, and Sue offered Emily a smile. The two of them slid into the front pew Emily first, then Jack, followed by Tyler, and finally Sue.

As the service began, the congregation filled the sanctuary with the familiar sounds of greetings, shuffling bulletins, and the soft rustle of pages. Pastor Raymin led the opening hymn, his voice strong as it echoed through the room.

When the time came for announcements, Pastor Raymin stepped forward with a warm smile. "Before we continue with the sermon, I have a special announcement. I am pleased to share that Jack and

Emily have decided to invite the entire congregation to join them for their wedding. With such a short time before the big day, they wanted to make sure no one was left out. The wedding will be held here at the church on January 16th, and everyone is welcome to attend and celebrate with them, please mark your calendar and join in the festivities!"

A soft murmur of delighted surprise and warm approval rippled through the congregation. Smiles and nods were exchanged, and several heads turned to look at Jack and Emily, seated in the front row.

Emily's cheeks flushed, and she offered a small, grateful wave. Jack gave a subtle nod, his heart light with gratitude for the support and shared joy of their church family.

As Pastor Raymin continued with the sermon, Tyler's hand shifted absentmindedly. He rested his arm on the back of the pew behind Sue, his fingers lightly brushing her shoulder. Gently, he eased her closer, her head leaning just slightly against his shoulder.

Emily glanced sideways, her lips curving into a quiet smile, and Jack followed her gaze, nodding approvingly. The connection between Tyler and Sue was not just a passing fancy it was something deeper, something built on kindness, faith, and the subtle guidance of the people around them.

As Pastor Raymin's words about love, faith, and community echoed through the sanctuary, their hearts stirred with gratitude. Jack squeezed Emily's hand, and she returned the gesture, her thoughts filled with the wedding, the community that surrounded them, and the quiet, steadfast love growing between the young couple at their side.

After the closing hymn, the congregation slowly filtered into the narthex, their voices blending in a low hum of conversation and laughter. Everyone seemed eager to offer congratulations to Jack and Emily, who stood near the doorway, shaking hands and exchanging smiles.

"Well done, you two!" one of the older ladies from the congregation said warmly. "It's so nice to see love blooming in the church."

A few others echoed similar sentiments, offering hugs and promises to attend the wedding. Emily felt her cheeks flush with gratitude and happiness as Jack wrapped a protective arm around her shoulders.

As the crowd began to thin, Sue appeared from the side, accompanied by a young woman with sandy blonde hair and a slightly shy smile. "Emily," Sue called as they approached, "I wanted to introduce you to Mary."

Emily turned, offering a warm smile. "Hi, Mary. It is nice to meet you."

Mary nodded, her hands clasped nervously. "Hi. It is nice to meet you too."

Sue placed a comforting hand on her friend's shoulder. "Mary's a good friend of mine. She is recently divorced she is only 25, no kids, but she is trying to get back on her feet. She lost her job at Walmart after the Christmas season ended, and she really needs something steady to help pay the rent. She worked in the electronics department, so she knows her way around the current music trends and ran the register. I thought she might be a good fit to help at the store, especially with everything coming up for the wedding and while you're in Nashville."

Emily's expression softened with understanding. She glanced at Mary, seeing the mixture of hope and apprehension in her eyes. "That is a wonderful idea. Sue, you will need help while I am away, and Mary sounds like she would be a great addition."

Mary's shoulders relaxed slightly, and she offered a faint smile. "Thank you. I really appreciate this opportunity. I was not sure what I was going to do next."

Emily smiled warmly. "Why don't you come by the store at nine on Monday morning? We will go over everything, and you can get a feel for the place."

Mary's eyes brightened, and she nodded. "I will be there. Thank you so much, Emily."

Sue grinned. "Thank you, Emily. This will make things so much easier, and I know Mary will do a wonderful job."

Jack, overhearing the conversation, added with a warm smile, "Sounds like everything's coming together."

Emily nodded, her heart full as she glanced between Jack, Sue, and Mary. "It really is."

As the last few churchgoers trickled out, the small group stood together in the narthex, sharing quiet laughter and anticipation for the busy days ahead, days filled with planning, faith, and the kind of community support that turned everyday challenges into shared triumphs.

The sanctuary had mostly emptied, and the lingering hum of quiet conversation faded into the narthex. Only a few members of the congregation stayed, mingling by the coat racks or sharing soft goodbyes at the doorway. Jack and Emily stood near the entrance, hands intertwined, receiving the last few congratulations.

"Well done, you two," one of the older ladies said with a knowing smile. "It's so lovely to see a wedding bring everyone together."

Emily's cheeks flushed, her heart warmed by the kindness of their church family. "Thank you. We could not imagine celebrating without everyone here."

Jack added with a nod, "We're grateful to be surrounded by such a supportive community."

Nearby, Sue and Mary stood together, quietly chatting and watching the happy exchanges. Mary's sandy blonde hair was pulled into a simple braid, and she looked noticeably lighter and more hopeful than she had a few days ago. She offered a small smile as Jack and Emily glanced over, and Sue gave her a gentle nudge.

"Mary's starting at the store tomorrow," Sue said, her voice brimming with quiet pride. "She's going to be such a help, especially with everything going on."

Emily nodded. "We are excited to have her. I think it is exactly the fresh start she needs."

It was then, with everyone gone and the narthex quiet except for the soft shuffle of a few departing footsteps, that Pastor Raymin approached the group. His usual warm expression was tinged with thoughtful gravity.

"I couldn't help but overhear," he said, his voice gentle as he glanced toward Mary. "So, you're starting at the store tomorrow, Mary?"

Mary nodded, her smile a little shy but genuine. "Yes, Pastor. Sue helped me get connected with Emily, and I will be starting in the morning."

Pastor Raymin's gaze softened as he looked at her with quiet understanding. "I'm glad to hear it. I have never liked divorce, as you all know. I believe in fighting for marriage whenever possible." He glanced at Jack and Emily, his tone low but sincere. "But I'll admit I don't disapprove of this one."

The group fell silent for a moment, listening intently as the pastor continued, his voice tinged with both sadness and reassurance.

"Mary's husband, Bill, used to be a good man. He was part of this church a solid Christian, always ready to lend a hand. But then he got into a fight at the mill lost his job, and everything changed. He stopped coming to church, started drinking heavily, and... he became mean. Angry. Someone none of us recognized anymore."

Mary's eyes glistened, but she stood tall, her hands clasped calmly in front of her. "I tried," she said quietly, her voice carrying the weight of her struggle. "I really tried, Pastor."

"I know you did," Pastor Raymin said gently. "Everyone who knew you both could see how hard you worked to keep things together. But there comes a time when staying is no longer the right thing, especially when there's no sign of repentance or change. Abuse is not part of the vows we make before God. It is not His plan for marriage."

Emily reached over and squeezed Mary's hand, her eyes warm and understanding.

Pastor Raymin smiled faintly. "You are still walking with the Lord, Mary. You have shown courage and grace in a challenging time, and I am glad you are finding support from friends like Sue and Emily. That is what community is about lifting each other up, offering hope when it feels like everything is falling apart."

Jack nodded in agreement, his voice steady and reassuring. "Mary's not alone now. We will make sure she is supported."

Sue beamed with quiet pride. "And I know she will be a blessing to the store. She has already got great ideas for reorganizing the new CD section."

Mary blushed, but her smile grew a little stronger. "I am excited to get started. Thank you all. I did not know what I was going to do before this, and now... I feel like I have a place again."

Emily's voice was warm and genuine. "We are glad to have you, Mary. You are part of the family now."

Pastor Raymin gave her a gentle nod. "I look forward to seeing you in church again. And I look forward to celebrating Jack and Emily's wedding with everyone. It is going to be a joyful day for all of us."

Jack and Emily shared a glance, their hearts full. Sue and Mary stepped a little closer, forming a small circle of friendship and support.

As the winter sunlight streamed through the stained-glass windows, the narthex was filled with quiet resilience and the promise of brighter days. Even in the face of hardship and heartbreak, love, faith, and community wove together into something enduring and strong.

And as the last of the churchgoers trickled out, leaving behind the soft echo of voices and the faint scent of old hymnals, Jack, Emily, Sue, and Mary stood together ready to face whatever came next with hope lighting their way.

Tyler who was just taking this all in said, "is my chauffeur ready to take me home? "

Sues face flushed with excitement and anticipation. "Only if you promise to behave yourself!"

Tyler said with a smirk, "who me!"

They all laughed as they went their separate ways.

# Chapter Six: A New Beginning

Monday morning dawned bright and cold, the sunlight bouncing off the icy patches on the sidewalk outside Pineville Record and Music Store. Emily unlocked the front door, her breath forming little clouds in the frosty air. Sue and Mary were right behind her, each bundled in warm coats and scarves, their cheeks pink from the chill.

Inside, the familiar scent of old records and fresh evergreen from the scents lingered in the air. Sue immediately made her way behind the counter, pulling off her gloves and setting them aside. "Let me get a pot of coffee going," she said cheerfully. "It's a good way to start the day."

"Sounds good," Emily said with a grin, holding the door open for Mary. "Come on in, Mary. Let us get you settled."

Mary stepped inside, her sandy blonde hair tucked neatly into a braid, her smile a mixture of nerves and excitement. "Thank you, Emily. I am so happy to be here."

Sue busied herself at the small coffee machine behind the counter, filling it with water and scooping in the ground beans. The soft drip and hiss of brewing coffee soon filled the air, adding a cozy warmth to the store.

Emily gestured for Mary to follow her, leading her around the front of the shop. "This is the main floor," she said, her tone friendly and encouraging. "We keep the CDs organized alphabetically by artist, and the newer releases are highlighted on these tables here. The vinyl collection's over in that corner mostly classic rock, country, and a few new artists. And the sheet music section is over there, popular with the local musicians."

Mary's eyes widened as she looked around, taking in the rows of gleaming CD cases, vinyl bins, and music books. "It's so organized," she said softly. "It looks like a lot to keep track of."

"It'll make sense soon enough," Emily reassured her. "Sue will walk you through everything, and she's great at explaining how things work around here."

The smell of brewing coffee drifted through the air as Sue returned with three steaming mugs. "Here you go," she said, handing one to Emily and one to Mary. "Best way to start a Monday morning."

"Thanks, Sue," Emily said, taking a grateful sip. "Perfect timing."

Mary cradled her mug between her hands, the warmth seeping into her fingers. "This is wonderful. Thank you."

Emily gestured toward the small counter with the register. "This is where you will spend a lot of your time. We handle cash, card, and checks here. It is a pretty simple system once you get the hang of it. Sue will give you the in-depth training today while I head back to the office to start your paperwork and background check."

Mary's smile faltered slightly, but Sue gave her a reassuring nod. "Don't worry. It's just the usual stuff. You'll do great."

"I hope so," Mary said quietly.

Emily placed a comforting hand on her shoulder. "I am sure everything will be fine. Let me know if you need anything while I am in the office."

With a final encouraging smile, Emily stepped through the door to the back office, closing it softly behind her.

Sue turned back to Mary, her tone light and cheerful. "All right, rookie. Let's dive in. We will start with the inventory. I will show you how we check stock and update the system on Monday mornings. It is not as complicated as it sounds."

They moved through the store, Sue showing how to cross-check the stock against the order list and how to restock new arrivals. "This list updates every Sunday night or first thing Monday," she explained. "It helps us keep track of what's selling and what we need to reorder."

Mary jotted down a few notes on a notepad Sue provided. "So, I'll need to check the list first thing every Monday?"

"Exactly," Sue said with a grin. "You're already getting the hang of it."

Back in the office, Emily sat at the small desk, sipping her coffee as she pulled up Mary's paperwork and background check. She entered Mary's information, her mind briefly wondering if any red flags would pop up. Moments later, the system confirmed everything was clear. Mary's record was clean, no issues in her past, except for a few remarks that were related to her and Bill, but nothing to keep her from working here. Emily allowed herself a small, relieved smile.

With the paperwork completed, she printed out the confirmation forms and placed them into a growing personnel file for Mary. She then turned to the vendor order reports, letting Sue handle the rest of Mary's training on the floor.

Out front, Sue guided Mary through the steps of handling returns, updating inventory, and even how to ring up a simple purchase at the register. The smell of fresh coffee still lingered, giving the store a comfortable, welcoming atmosphere.

A customer wandered in, a middle-aged man in a worn leather jacket. "Morning, ladies," he said with a nod. "Looking for the new Luke Bryan album. You got it?"

Sue glanced at Mary and gave her a nudge. "Go ahead, Mary. Take the lead."

Mary hesitated, then nodded. "Let me check for you," she said, pulling up the inventory on the register. After a moment, she smiled. "Yes, we have two copies left. Right over here."

She led the man to the display table, handed him the album, and processed the sale smoothly at the counter. When he left, she turned to Sue, her eyes shining with pride. "That wasn't so bad."

"Told you," Sue said with a wink. "You're a natural."

Emily returned from the office a few minutes later, smiling as she observed Mary restocking shelves while Sue double-checked the order list.

"How's it going out here?" Emily asked, stepping behind the counter.

"Really well," Sue said, her voice warm and approving. "Mary's a quick learner."

Mary smiled, her confidence visibly growing. "I feel a lot more comfortable than I did this morning."

Emily handed her the completed paperwork. "Here is your folder and a copy of your background check all clear. Welcome to the team, Mary."

Mary's hands trembled slightly as she accepted the papers. "Thank you. I really appreciate this opportunity."

Sue gave her a playful nudge. "Told you Emily's good people."

The three of them shared a warm laugh as the sunlight streamed through the front windows, casting a glow over the shelves of music and the beginnings of a new chapter for Mary.

As the clock on the wall edged toward eleven, the quiet hum of the music store continued. Sue and Mary were finishing a small restock when Emily's voice called from the back office.

"Mary? Could you step in for a moment?"

Mary froze, her hands tightening around a stack of CDs. Her pulse quickened as all sorts of anxious thoughts tumbled through her mind. Had something come up? Did Emily find something bad in the background check? Was she going to lose the job she had barely begun?

Sue noticed her hesitation and gave her a gentle smile. "Don't worry, it is just paperwork or something simple. You are doing great. Go ahead."

Mary swallowed hard, offering a faint smile in return. "Okay... I hope so."

With tentative steps, she made her way to the office, her thoughts spinning. She thought of her ex-husband, Bill, of her past struggles, of the fear she had carried for so long. Could something from her past have followed her here?

Mary stepped inside, her hands clenched nervously. The office was small but welcoming, with a neatly stacked desk, a gently steaming mug of coffee, and a faint scent of paper and ink. Emily sat behind the desk, her expression kind and encouraging.

"Have a seat," Emily said, gesturing to the chair across from her.

Mary sat, her shoulders tight with apprehension. "Is everything okay?" she asked softly.

Emily's smile was steady and reassuring. "Everything's fine, Mary. No need to worry. I just wanted to have a quick chat with you nothing bad, I promise."

Mary let out a shaky breath, her hands loosening in her lap. "Oh... I was afraid something might be wrong."

Emily chuckled gently. "I understand. It's natural to feel nervous. But you're doing a fantastic job, and I could not be happier to have you here. That's why I wanted to talk to you about your job and make sure you feel valued."

Mary sat up a little straighter, her hands still resting on her lap. "I really appreciate this opportunity, Emily. It means so much to me."

Emily nodded. "That's exactly why I wanted to ask you a few things." She glanced down at a notepad on her desk. "First, if you don't mind me asking, how much was Walmart paying you, and how many hours were you working there?"

Mary hesitated but answered truthfully. "I was making eleven dollars an hour, but they never gave me more than thirty-two hours a week. No benefits, just enough to barely scrape by."

Emily's lips pressed together thoughtfully. "That's what I suspected. And your rent how much is it?"

Mary's cheeks flushed, and she glanced down at her hands. "It's six hundred a month," she admitted quietly. "And payday is only three days before the rent's due. I wasn't sure how I was going to make it this month. I didn't want to say anything because... well, I'm just grateful for the job."

Emily's heart ached at the vulnerability in Mary's voice. She leaned forward, her tone firm but kind. "Mary, you don't need to be afraid to speak up. That's what I'm here for. I want to help." She took a breath, her mind already made up. "Here is what we are going to do. I am offering you twelve dollars an hour, full-time forty hours a week. And we are adding health benefits. I want to make sure you are covered and stable."

Mary's eyes widened, her breath catching. "Really? Full-time and benefits?"

Emily nodded with a smile. "Yes. But I'm not done. I'm going to help with your rent this month. I will pay the six hundred upfront, so you are not scrambling before payday. After that, I will withhold forty dollars from each paycheck until the balance is repaid. That way, you can focus on settling in and not worry about making rent three days after payday."

For a long moment, Mary was too stunned to respond. Her mouth opened slightly, her eyes shimmering with unshed tears. "You'd really do that for me?"

"Of course," Emily said softly. "You deserve a fresh start, Mary. You have been through enough already. This is a chance for you to stand on your own feet without being overwhelmed."

Tears welled in Mary's eyes, and she wiped them quickly with the back of her hand. "Thank you, Emily. I... I don't even know what to say. I thought I was going to lose everything. I thought I would have to move out because I could not make rent."

Emily reached across the desk, resting her hand gently over Mary's. "You are not alone anymore. You have support here. You have Sue, you have me, and soon you will have health insurance too. This is not just a job, Mary. It is a family."

Mary nodded, her lips trembling into a grateful smile. "I won't let you down. I promise. I will work hard, and I will make sure you can count on me."

"I already do," Emily said with a soft laugh. "And you have a good teacher in Sue. The two of you will make a wonderful team."

They sat there for a few more moments, the weight of Emily's offer settling like a warm embrace. For the first time in what felt like forever, Mary felt a genuine spark of hope. She was not scraping by on a threadbare paycheck. She was not holding her breath every month, praying she could cover rent. She had a plan a path forward and a community willing to lift her up.

Finally, Emily stood, smoothing the papers on her desk. "Go back out there with Sue. There is still plenty to do today. And Mary," she added, her smile gentle, "you're going to be just fine."

Mary stood as well, her steps lighter than they had been that morning. "Thank you, Emily. This means everything to me."

Emily nodded. "I am glad. Now go out there and show Sue what you are made of."

"Emily" Mary said, "Is it okay to give the boss a hug?"

With that Emily moved forward and embraced Mary. To Mary she finally felt warmth, love, and a family type feeling!

As Mary rejoined Sue on the sales floor, her heart felt light for the first time in months. And as the music played softly through the speakers, the quiet comfort of knowing she was finally, truly, starting over wrapped around her like a warm embrace

The afternoon sun was casting long, warm rays across the front windows of the record store as Emily stepped out of the office, phone still in hand and a determined but cheerful expression on her face. She spotted Sue and Mary by the register, double-checking stock on a clipboard.

"Hey, ladies," Emily called out, drawing their attention. "Quick update just got off the phone with the bridal shop in the next town. They had an unexpected cancellation, so I grabbed the 3:30 slot for today."

Sue raised an eyebrow, glancing at the wall clock. "That's going to cut it close, isn't it?"

Emily nodded. "Yeah, it is. I will need to close the shop by three so we can make it on time. Sue, would you mind walking Mary through the closing procedures today?"

Sue grinned. "Of course. We will start closing things down around 2:30 so I can show her everything. Mary, it is not as hard as it sounds, and it will give you a good sense of how we wrap things up at the end of the day."

Mary glanced between them, a bit surprised. "Is that something that happens often?"

Sue laughed softly. "Every now and then. With small businesses, we sometimes adjust our hours for appointments or dedicated events. Especially now with Emily's wedding coming up, there will be a few more schedule changes than usual."

Mary nodded, her nerves beginning to ease. "That makes sense. I am ready to learn."

Emily smiled, her tone light. "Good, because tomorrow we're also closing early."

Mary's brows lifted. "Oh? Another appointment?"

Sue grinned, nudging Mary playfully. "Not quite. Tomorrow we are closing at three again, but this time for a special reason Tyler's birthday party. We are throwing a little pizza party right here at the store after closing. You are more than welcome to join us."

Mary's face lit up, her smile genuine and warm. "That sounds wonderful. Thank you for inviting me."

"Of course," Emily said. "It will be a wonderful way to celebrate Tyler's birthday, even if it is a day late. And it will give everyone a chance to relax a little and have some fun together."

Sue glanced at the clipboard in her hand. "All right let's start going over the closing process now. I will show you how we reconcile the register, prep the bank deposit, restock a few of the displays, and reset the store for the next day. It sounds like a lot, but it's straightforward once you've done it a couple of times."

Mary nodded, her hands steady and her heart lighter than it had been in months. "I'm ready."

They worked side by side as Emily prepared for her bridal appointment, Sue showing Mary how to count the cash drawer, balance the totals against the day's sales, and fill out the deposit slip. "We'll go over this again tomorrow too," Sue said. "But it's always better to have a couple of practice runs before you're doing it on your own."

Mary followed each step carefully, asking questions and jotting down notes. By the time they finished reviewing the process, the store felt like a second home a place where she belonged.

As Emily checked her phone one last time and confirmed her appointment details, she glanced over at Mary and Sue. "Thanks again, both of you. I will feel a lot better knowing things are covered here today and tomorrow. And Mary, I really hope you will join us for the pizza party. It will be nice for you to meet a few more people and for us to all celebrate together."

"I'll definitely be there," Mary said, her smile steady and her heart full of gratitude.

With that, the day wound down not with uncertainty but with a comforting sense of community, support, and the promise of new beginnings. The quiet rhythm of the record store continued until 2:30, when they began their end-of-day routine, preparing for Emily's appointment and the pizza party the next afternoon where laughter, friendship, and music would fill the space once more.

As the day wore on, the hum of activity in the record store settled into a steady rhythm. Mary followed Sue through the closing procedures, learning how to reconcile the register, count cash, restock shelves, and tidy up for the next day.

"See? It's not so hard," Sue said with a wink as she handed Mary the key to the cash drawer. "Once you have done it a couple of times, it becomes second nature. The important thing is to stay organized and double-check the totals. If something is off, we will catch it before the deposit gets made."

Mary nodded, her brow furrowed in concentration as she carefully counted the bills. "I think I'm getting the hang of it. Thank you for showing me everything today. It has been a lot to take in, but it is fun."

Sue grinned. "Told you it would be. Besides, once we close and head home, you will feel like you have really accomplished something."

They continued working side by side, the clock on the wall inching closer to 3:00. Mary felt a surprising sense of pride as she finished logging the day's transactions and helped Sue restock the new release table. The weight of her worries about rent, her past, and starting over had lightened as she focused on the simple tasks and the friendly atmosphere.

At precisely three o'clock, Emily appeared from the back office, her coat already draped over her arm and a stack of paperwork organized in her hands. "All right, ladies, time to lock up. We have to hit the road if we are going to make my bridal appointment on time."

Sue gave a playful salute. "Aye aye, boss. Everything is ready for a smooth close."

Mary turned the sign on the front door to "Closed" and helped Sue switch off the overhead lights. Together, they tidied the last few items on the counter and wiped down the glass display case. Emily double-checked the cash totals against the deposit slip and handed Sue the bank bag.

"Great job today, both of you," Emily said with a satisfied nod. "Mary, you did fantastic for your first day. I'm glad you are here."

Mary's cheeks flushed with gratitude. "Thank you. I am so grateful for this opportunity. It feels good to be part of something again."

Emily's smile softened. "You're more than part of something you're part of the family now."

Sue grinned, nudging Mary gently. "Speaking of family, don't forget tomorrow we're closing early again for Tyler's birthday party. We'll set everything up right here at the store. You will come, right?"

Mary nodded. "Of course. I would not miss it."

As they gathered their things and Emily locked the front door behind them, Mary hesitated, glancing at Sue with a playful but curious expression.

"Hey, Sue?" she asked, her voice light and teasing.

Sue turned, raising an eyebrow. "Yeah?"

Mary grinned. "Why do you keep talking about Tyler so much? Every time I turn around, you are mentioning him. Is there something I should know?"

Sue froze for just a moment, her cheeks coloring faintly, but she recovered with a mock-serious expression. "What? Me? Talking about Tyler? Pfft, I do not know what you are talking about," she said, waving her hand dramatically.

Mary laughed softly, shaking her head. "Come on. It is obvious. You two seem close."

Sue rolled her eyes playfully but could not hide the slight flush creeping up her neck. "Fine. I've mentioned him a few times. More than a few. It's just... he's a good guy, you know? And well... he's Tyler. He's kind, funny, and... oh, I don't know. I just like him a little more than I thought I did."

Mary's smile widened. "A little more, huh?"

Sue groaned, covering her face with her hands. "Okay, fine! I like him a lot. Happy now?"

Mary laughed, her earlier nerves forgotten. "Don't worry. Your secret's safe with me. Besides, he is great too. You two would make a cute couple."

Sue peeked between her fingers, her face warming. "You think so?"

"Definitely," Mary said with a grin. "But do not worry I will keep my matchmaking instincts to myself. For now."

Sue groaned again but could not help laughing as they continued toward Emily's car in the crisp air. Emily joined them a moment later, locking the door behind her and pocketing the keys.

"Ready to head out?" Emily asked, glancing at Sue and Mary.

"Yep," Sue said, her voice bright. "Let's hit the road."

With the shop closed and the evening ahead, the three women walked toward their cars, the warmth of friendship and the promise of new beginnings lingering in the air.

As Mary climbed into her car, she couldn't help but smile. For the first time in a long while, she felt hopeful. She had a job she loved, people who cared about her, and even just maybe the chance to be part of something bigger than herself.

And with tomorrow's pizza party to look forward to, she knew this was only the beginning.

# Chapter Seven: Dresses and Tuxedos

As Emily fastened her seatbelt and started the car, Sue climbed into the passenger seat, her cheeks still flushed with excitement from Mary's first day at the shop. The afternoon sun sparkled on the windshield, and Emily couldn't help but smile as she pulled out her phone.

"I'm just going to call Jack really quick and let him know we're heading to the bridal shop," she said, glancing at Sue. "I'll put him on speaker so you can hear too."

Sue nodded eagerly, her own excitement bubbling just beneath the surface.

Emily tapped Jack's contact and waited as the phone rang. It only took a few seconds before his familiar voice picked up, warm and easy.

"Hey there, beautiful. Everything all right at the store?" Jack's voice came through the speaker, making Sue grin and Emily's heart lift.

"Hi, sweetheart," Emily said, her smile audible. "Just letting you know Sue and I are on our way to the bridal shop. They had an opening for this afternoon, so we are going to see if we can find my dress today."

"Sounds great," Jack replied. "Actually, funny you called. Tyler and I are at the tuxedo shop now, I picked him up after school!"

Emily's eyes widened, her hand tightening slightly on the steering wheel. "You did? How is it going?"

Jack chuckled. "Really well. The guy at the shop is super nice, said he is glad it's January and not wedding season because he has the time to help us out. He is going to have the peach shirts for us, just like we wanted."

Sue let out a little cheer. "Peach shirts! Perfect!"

Emily laughed. "That is fantastic, Jack. When will the tuxedo be ready?"

"The guy said he'd have them ready by the thirteenth," Jack replied, the satisfaction clear in his voice. "He said it was lucky we caught him now before things pick up with spring weddings. He even offered to call me when they come in so we can get fitted early if we want."

Emily's heart lightened. "That's amazing. Everything is coming together."

"It really is," Jack said, his voice warm. "You find yourself the perfect dress, okay? And tell Sue she's not allowed to let you settle for anything less than what makes you feel like a queen."

Emily's cheeks flushed with happiness. "I'll hold her to that."

Sue grinned. "Don't worry, Jack. I've got this."

Jack laughed softly. "Good. And Mary I said she is doing a wonderful job at the store. Tyler was impressed with her too when we stopped by earlier."

"I will," Emily said, her heart full. "Thanks, love. I'll call you later and tell you how it goes."

"Sounds perfect. I'll see you at home," Jack replied. "Love you."

"Love you too," Emily said softly.

Sue gave Emily a playful nudge as they ended the call. "Well, sounds like the guys got their tuxes figured out."

Emily nodded, her eyes shining. "Yeah, they did. And now it is our turn to make sure the dress is just as perfect."

As she turned onto the highway leading to the next town, Emily felt a sense of excitement building. The wedding plans were falling into place, piece by piece, and with each step, it all felt more joyful.

She glanced at Sue, her smile wide and hopeful. "Let's go find my dream dress."

As Emily merged onto the two-lane road out of Pineville, she glanced at the clock on the dashboard and sighed. "We're going to be a few minutes late," she said, pulling out her phone.

Sue's eyebrows rose as Emily tapped the contact for the bridal shop. "Think they'll hold the appointment?"

Emily put the call on speaker as the line rang twice before a friendly voice answered. "Brook Stone Bridal, how can I help you?"

"Hi, this is Emily," she said, her tone a mix of apologetic and cheerful. "We're on our way for the 3:30 appointment, but we're running a few minutes late. Just wanted to give you a heads-up."

The woman on the other end chuckled. "No worries at all, Emily. Just get here safe and don't pick up any speeding tickets!"

Emily laughed, exchanging a glance with Sue. "Thank you! We will be there soon."

As she ended the call, she relaxed slightly, tapping her fingers lightly on the steering wheel. "At least they are not stressed about the timing. They just told me to drive safe and not get any tickets."

Sue grinned. "That's good. And it's not like you're in a rush to get arrested on the way to your dress fitting."

Emily snorted. "Please. we are still in Pineville; I am not too worried. I know the local police here. I could get away with a warning if I was going a little over."

Sue's mouth dropped open in mock shock. "Emily!"

Emily laughed, shaking her head. "I am joking mostly. But yes, I know a few of the officers. Small-town rewards. Still, I would not push it too much."

They continued down the familiar stretch of road, the sun slanting low through the trees. As they approached the sign welcoming them into Brook Stone, Emily's humor faded into determination.

"Okay, now we're entering Brook Stone," she said, her tone turning serious. "This is where Jack got his black belt, and I do not want to mess around here. Their police are... let us just say, not as lenient as Pineville's."

Sue laughed. "So, you're saying, now's the time to obey the speed limit like a model citizen?"

"Exactly," Emily said with a grin. "I am not risking a ticket this close to finding my dream dress. Besides, Jack would never let me hear the end of it if I got pulled over in his old stomping grounds."

Sue chuckled. "Fair enough. We will play it safe."

Emily eased her foot off the accelerator as they drove through the more polished streets of Brook Stone, lined with boutique shops and cafes. The bridal shop's address was keyed into the GPS, and she followed the turns carefully, glancing at the speedometer every few seconds to ensure she stayed well within the limit.

"Almost there," Sue said, leaning forward to look out the windshield. "I think that's the shop up ahead."

Emily's nerves fluttered with excitement. "Let's go find that perfect dress."

They pulled into the small parking lot of Brook Stone Bridal at exactly 3:38 p.m. Emily let out a breath of relief as she parked. "See? We made it. Just a few minutes late."

Sue grinned as they stepped out into the chilly air. "And no speeding tickets. I call that a win."

The shop's bell jingled as they entered. Inside, the boutique was cozy and filled with soft light, its walls lined with elegant gowns shimmering in shades of ivory and white.

A smiling consultant in a crisp, pale pink blouse approached them immediately. "Welcome to Brook Stone Bridal! I'm Marissa. You must be Emily?"

"Yes," Emily said, returning the smile as she extended her hand. "Sorry we're a few minutes late. We got caught up with work, but we are here now."

Marissa shook her hand warmly. "No worries at all. We are glad you made it. And you must be Sue?" she added, turning to Sue with a welcoming nod.

"That's me," Sue said, her eyes already scanning the rows of gowns.

"Well, come on in," Marissa said, gesturing toward a comfortable seating area near the fitting rooms. "Do you have an idea of what you're looking for today, Emily?"

Emily took a deep breath, her expression calm but resolute. "Yes, I do. I am a faithful Christian, so I am looking for something conservative. No cleavage or truly little showing. Shoulders can be exposed, but nothing too flashy. Full-length dress, of course. And the veil I want it to be shorter than the dress. I can be clumsy sometimes, and I do not want to trip over it walking down the aisle."

Marissa's face lit with understanding and respect. "That is wonderful to know, Emily. We have several options that match those preferences. You will be surprised at how many beautiful gowns offer a modest yet elegant look. Let us look at a few styles and see what catches your eye."

Sue gave Emily an encouraging smile. "That's a great description, Em. You'll find something perfect."

Emily followed Marissa toward a rack of gowns, feeling a mixture of nervousness and anticipation. The dresses hung in graceful lines, some shimmering with delicate beadwork, others flowing with soft, unadorned fabrics.

Marissa ran her hand lightly over a few gowns, selecting several that matched Emily's criteria. "Here is one with cap sleeves and a lace overlay very classic and conservative. This one has a higher neckline and a beautiful A-line skirt, and this one features a simple satin design with a slightly lowered back but still modest."

Emily's fingers brushed over the fabrics, feeling the weight and texture of each dress. "These are lovely," she said softly. "I'd love to try them on."

"Of course," Marissa said, leading her toward the fitting rooms. "Let me get these set up for you. Take your time and let me know how each one feels. We will find the perfect dress for your big day."

Sue settled into one of the chairs near the large mirror, ready to offer her honest opinions and supportive encouragement. "Don't worry, Emily. We will make sure you feel like a queen without tripping down the aisle."

Emily laughed, her nerves easing a bit. "Thanks, Sue. I'll need all the help I can get."

As Marissa disappeared into the back to prepare the first gown, Emily glanced at her reflection in the large mirror, her heart fluttering with anticipation. This was really happening. The dress, the wedding it was all coming together. And though she felt a bit clumsy and overwhelmed, she knew she was surrounded by people who loved and supported her every step of the way.

Emily stepped out of the fitting room in the first gown Marissa had suggested. It was elegant, with delicate lace cap sleeves and a flowing A-line skirt. Sue's face lit with appreciation as Emily turned in front of the mirror.

"It's beautiful," Sue said, leaning forward to admire the detail.

Emily smiled but shook her head. "It is, but... I don't know. It just doesn't feel quite right."

Marissa nodded knowingly. "That's completely normal. Let's try the next one."

The second dress featured a high neckline and intricate beadwork, the satin material shimmering softly under the shop's lights. Emily stepped out, smoothing her hands over the fabric, her expression thoughtful.

Sue tilted her head, considering. "This one is too. Very classic."

Emily turned from side to side in the mirror, studying the lines and the fit. "It is nice, but... still not it. It is just missing something."

She was about to step back into the fitting room when a glimpse of color in the far corner of the shop caught her eye. Her breath caught as she stepped closer, her gaze drawn to a gown unlike any other she'd seen. It was a mixture of soft white and delicate peach, the lace overlay blending the two colors into a subtle, romantic design.

"Oh," Emily whispered, her fingers brushing the fabric. "Marissa, can I try this one?"

Marissa's eyes widened with surprise. "Of course! That's one of our unique designs' part of a limited collection. I'll get it ready for you right away."

Sue grinned from her chair. "That peach in the lace... it will match the guys' shirts perfectly. It is like it was meant for you."

Emily slipped into the gown with Marissa's assistance, the fabric settling over her frame with surprising ease. When she stepped out and faced the mirror, her breath caught. The blend of white and peach complemented her complexion beautifully, the modest neckline with the lace covering her and flowing skirt adding an understated elegance that made her heart flutter.

Sue's eyes widened with delight. "Emily... that's the one."

Emily turned slowly, her reflection shimmering softly. "It is, isn't it?" she said, her voice quiet with awe. "It's perfect. It even ties in with what the guys will be wearing."

Marissa beamed. "It is absolutely stunning on you. And we will make sure it fits perfectly for the big day."

As Emily changed back into her clothes, Marissa stepped over to Sue. "Are you in the wedding party?" she asked, her tone casual.

Sue nodded, a little surprised. "Yes, I am the maid of honor. Why?"

Marissa's eyes lit up. "We had a cancellation for a bridesmaid's dress in a size close to yours. The best part? It is entirely peach matches perfectly with the accents on Emily's dress and the groomsmen's shirts. If you are interested, you could try it on today, and we can finish both dresses at once."

Sue's mouth dropped open slightly. "Are you serious?"

"Absolutely," Marissa said with a grin. "Let me grab it."

A few minutes later, Sue stepped out of the fitting room in the peach gown, her cheeks glowing. The dress fit her perfectly, the color a soft, warm peach that complemented her skin tone and matched Emily's gown perfectly.

Emily clapped her hands together, her heart soaring. "Sue, you look beautiful. This is perfect!"

Sue laughed, her voice light with joy. "It really is. It is like God lined this up just for us."

Marissa nodded. "Both dresses look fantastic. I will schedule your final fittings for the 14th, so everything is perfect for the big day."

Emily hugged Sue tightly. "This is really happening. It is all coming together."

They left the bridal shop, their arms linked and their hearts full. As Emily navigated the familiar roads back toward Pineville, Sue glanced over at her, a soft smile playing on her lips.

"You know," she said thoughtfully, "God's hand is in all of this. Everything is falling into place the dresses, the tuxedos, the timing. It is like He is guiding us each step of the way."

Emily glanced at her, her eyes shining with gratitude. "I think you're right. And it makes me even more excited for the wedding, knowing we're surrounded by so much love and support."

They drove on in quiet, contented anticipation, the soft glow of the setting sun casting long shadows across the road. As the miles passed, they talked about final fittings, pizza parties, and the joyful days to come confident that with faith and friendship, everything was exactly as it should be.

# Chapter Eight: Cake Plans and Store Chats

The morning air was crisp and clear as Mary stood waiting outside the Pineville Record and Music Store. She shifted her weight from one foot to the other, glancing up at the familiar sign above the door. It would be a few more days before she could get her own key, so for now, she waited for Emily or Sue to arrive.

A few minutes later, Emily and Sue pulled into the parking lot, stepping out of Emily's car with warm smiles and shopping bags in tow.

"Morning, Mary!" Emily called cheerfully as she unlocked the front door.

Mary grinned. "Good morning! I am ready to learn more today."

As soon as the door clicked open, Mary dashed inside, heading straight for the coffee pot on the counter. "I definitely need to learn how to use this," she said with a laugh.

Emily and Sue burst into laughter, following her inside. "That's the spirit!" Sue said, her voice light and teasing. "Coffee is an essential part of running this place."

Emily smiled as she set the bags down by the counter. "Do not worry, Mary. I will show you how the coffee maker works before the day's out."

Once the laughter settled, Mary glanced at the shopping bags. "So... how'd it go with the dresses yesterday?" she asked, her eyes sparkling with curiosity.

Emily's face lit up with excitement. "It was amazing. I found the perfect gown a blend of white and peach lace that is elegant but modest. It ties in perfectly with the guys' peach shirts. And guess what? Sue found a last-minute bridesmaid dress in all peach. It was like it was meant to be."

Sue nodded enthusiastically. "It was like the dress was waiting for me. I cannot wait to show it off at the wedding."

Mary's smile widened. "That is incredible. I am so happy for you both. It sounds like everything is falling into place."

Emily glanced at the clock, her mind already shifting into planning mode. "All right, you two keep opening. I will head back to the office to take care of a few things, and I will call the bakery to schedule a cake consultation for later today."

"Sounds good," Sue said as she and Mary moved to restock the new release table and double-check the inventory sheets.

Emily made her way into the small office, settling into the chair behind the desk. She pulled out her phone and dialed the bakery's number, her voice warm and professional when the line connected.

"Hi, this is Emily from the record store down the street. I would like to make an appointment for a cake consultation around noon today, if possible."

There was a pause on the other end, followed by a cheerful response. "Absolutely! Noon works perfectly. We will see you then."

"Thank you so much," Emily said, ending the call with a satisfied smile.

She glanced out into the store where Sue and Mary were working together, their easy laughter and teamwork filling the space with energy. Everything was coming together one small step at a time.

As Mary and Sue continued with the morning routine stocking shelves, checking the inventory list, and tidying up a few customers trickled into the store. The front bell jingled lightly, and a pair of women wandered in, browsing the new release table. Not long after, an older man stepped through the door, looking around curiously.

"I've got the ladies," Sue said to Mary with a grin, grabbing a basket of CDs to straighten nearby. "Why don't you see what the gentleman needs?"

Mary's heart gave a small flutter of nerves, but she squared her shoulders and approached the man with a friendly smile. "Good morning! Can I help you find anything today?"

The man turned, his face lighting up. "Actually, yes. I am looking for a new country album for my wife she loves George Strait. Do you have any of his latest CDs?"

"Absolutely," Mary said, leading him to the proper section. "We just got a shipment of his newest release last week. Here it is."

The man beamed as he took the CD from her hands. "Perfect. She is going to love this. Thank you so much."

"Happy to help," Mary said, ringing up his purchase as Sue chatted with the two women by the new releases. Moments later, the customers left with cheerful goodbyes and full shopping bags.

As the door closed behind them, Emily appeared from the office, her phone still in hand. "Well, ladies, I made the noon appointment with the bakery for the cake tasting." She turned to Mary, her voice full of quiet confidence. "You will be fine here while Sue and I head over. We will only be two doors down if you need us."

Mary's cheeks flushed with pride. "Thank you, Emily. I will be fine. I have this."

Sue added with a grin, "We will be back before you know it. And hey, you handled that customer like a pro."

Mary smiled, her confidence growing.

Emily glanced at the clock and then at her phone. "Before we get too far into the morning rush, how about we order something to eat? I will DoorDash from McDonald's and have it here by 11:30. That way we can eat between customers and before heading to the bakery."

Sue's face lit up. "That sounds perfect. I will take a Big Mac combo with a Coke, please."

Mary laughed softly, her stomach rumbling at the thought. "I'll go with a McChicken sandwich and fries, Diet Coke for me."

"Got it," Emily said, tapping in the order. "Big Mac combo for Sue, McChicken, and fries for Mary, and I will just get a salad with a medium Coke. This way we are not starving when we meet with the bakery."

As Emily finished the order, she looked up with a grin. "All right, foods on the way. Let us keep things rolling until lunchtime, and then we will handle cake business."

With the promise of food and the excitement of wedding plans, the trio settled back into their rhythm, ready to tackle the day.

Sue chuckled as she glanced at Emily. "That was a great idea ordering lunch before the bakery you never want to go to a bakery hungry."

They all laughed, and Emily grinned. "You are right. I certainly do not need to add any extra weight before the wedding!"

Before heading to the bakery, Emily pulled out her phone and scrolled to Pastor Raymin's contact. She tapped to call, and after a few rings, his familiar voice answered warmly.

"Hi, Pastor, it's Emily," she said. "I just wanted to ask how many people do you think we should plan for at the wedding? I am ordering the cake today and I need an estimate."

Pastor Raymin chuckled. "Since it is you and Jack, I would say expect around 400. It is going to be a big celebration, and you know how everyone loves to turn out for weddings." Pastor started coughing.

Emily's eyes widened as she exchanged a glance with Sue. "Wow, okay. Thanks, Pastor. I will plan for that. And Pastor take something for that cough!"

They made their way to the bakery, just two doors down from the record store. The warm, sweet scent of baking bread and frosting greeted them as they entered.

A cheerful baker in a white apron welcomed them. "Hi there! You must be here for the cake consultation."

"That's us," Emily said, shaking the baker's hand. "I am Emily, and this is Sue. We are planning a white and peach-colored wedding, and we were thinking of something elegant but simple."

Sue added with a smile, "And we just found out we should plan for about 400 guests."

The baker nodded thoughtfully. "Got it. For that many people, I would recommend a three-tier cake for the main display and then a couple of sheet cakes for serving."

"That sounds perfect," Emily said. "We'd like the colors to match the wedding white with peach accents."

The baker jotted down notes, sketching a quick design with delicate peach flowers and a satin-smooth white icing. "We can deliver everything on the morning of the wedding and set it up at the reception hall."

Emily smiled, feeling the plans falling into place. "That would be wonderful. Thank you so much."

Sue grinned as they wrapped up the appointment. "Looks like the cake's handled.

As Emily and Sue stepped out of the bakery, the scent of sugar and fresh bread still lingering in the air, Emily glanced across the street toward the small flower shop. The display of vibrant blooms caught her eye, and she noticed there were not any customers inside.

"Hey," Emily said, nudging Sue's arm. "The flower shop is not busy. What do you say we pop in and handle the flowers and the bridal bouquets while we're at it?"

Sue's face brightened. "That's a great idea! Might as well knock out two things today. Let's do it."

They crossed the street, stepping into the cozy shop filled with the fragrance of fresh flowers. A cheerful florist behind the counter looked up from arranging a vase of delicate white roses.

"Good afternoon, ladies! How can I help you today?"

Emily smiled. "Hi! We are planning a wedding white and peach colors, and we would like to place an order for the wedding flowers and my bridal bouquet."

Sue added, "And we're thinking we should settle the order now since we're already out and about."

The florist's eyes lit up with excitement. "Perfect! Let us sit down and go over the details. I will help you plan something beautiful for your big day."

Emily smiled at the florist as she and Sue took seats at the small consultation table. "The wedding is on the 16th," she said. "We are going with a white and peach color scheme. I would love to have peach roses and white roses for the bouquets and arrangements."

The florist nodded enthusiastically, jotting down notes. "A classic and beautiful combination. We can create a bridal bouquet of mixed peach and white roses, with coordinating arrangements for the church and reception. Did you want matching flowers for the bridesmaids and boutonnieres for the groomsmen as well?"

"Yes, please," Emily said. "Sue's dress is peach, so a bouquet with more white roses and just a touch of peach will match beautifully. And for the boutonnieres, let us do simple white roses with a peach ribbon."

Sue grinned. "That sounds perfect."

The florist made a few quick sketches to show the layout of the floral arrangements. "We'll deliver and set everything up on the morning of the 16th," she said. "You're going to love it."

"Thank you so much," Emily said, standing up and shaking the florist's hand. "I'm excited to see it all come together."

With the flower order placed, Emily and Sue made their way back to the music store. The afternoon sun was still high, casting warm light across the sidewalk. As they stepped through the door, Mary greeted them with a wave from behind the counter.

"Hey, welcome back! How'd it go?" Mary asked, her face lighting up with curiosity.

Sue set her purse on the counter with a satisfied smile. "We got the cake and flowers taken care of. Everything is really coming together."

Emily nodded, her voice light with relief. "Now we just need to finish out the afternoon and get ready for Tyler's birthday party later."

Mary's eyes sparkled. "I'll help with whatever you need."

The three women shared a smile as they settled back into the familiar rhythm of the store, preparing for a day filled with music, planning, and soon, pizza and celebration.

# Chapter Nine: Tyler's Best Birthday Ever

At 2:45 p.m., just as the afternoon light was starting to turn golden through the store windows, Jack stepped inside the record store, brushing a bit of road dust from his jacket. He spotted Mary at the counter and gave her a warm smile.

"Hey, Mary. How's everything going today?" he asked.

Mary straightened up, beaming with pride. "Really good, Jack. We've been busy, but everything is under control. Emily and Sue handled the bakery and flower appointments earlier, and we have been getting ready for Tyler's birthday party."

Just then, Emily walked over from the back, grinning. "Hey, Jack. Just so you know, I have been spending your royalty check on flowers and cakes today."

Jack burst out laughing, wrapping an arm around her. "That is exactly what it is for making sure everything is perfect for you. And for Tyler's party, of course."

At 2:55, the door swung open again, and Tyler walked in, his eyes scanning the store until they landed on Sue. His face lit up as he strode over to her, wrapping his arms around her in a warm hug. "I've missed you," he murmured.

Sue blushed, returning the hug. "I missed you too, Tyler. How was school today?"

Tyler said with a grin, "I got an A on the history exam! My life has certainly turned around thanks to the help of dad, I mean Jack!"

Jack heard that, "Tyler, I think of you as a son and if you want to call me dad, I would be honored."

Within minutes, more people arrived the familiar faces of Tyler's gang from school, the pastor and his wife Marcy, a few girls from the karate class, and even a couple of loyal customers who had become friends.

Emily noticed the pastor, "Pastor, are you feeling okay, you look off?"

"I just haven't felt the best and have thus cold" he replied

The store filled with laughter, chatter, and the scent of pizza as boxes were delivered and set up on the back counter.

Emily clapped her hands to get everyone's attention. "All right, everyone! Before we dig into the pizza, I have something special for Tyler's birthday."

She turned to him, her eyes twinkling, and handed him a small, wrapped box. "Happy birthday, Tyler. This is from me."

Tyler unwrapped it quickly, revealing a brand-new cell phone a contract phone with a one-year unlimited use plan. His eyes widened in surprise and delight.

"Wow, Emily! This is amazing! Thank you so much!" he exclaimed, turning the phone over in his hands.

Emily smiled. "You'll need it to keep in touch with Sue and to call us when you head off to Nashville after graduation."

As everyone clapped and cheered, Jack disappeared into the small storage closet at the back of the store. A moment later, he appeared, carrying a sleek new guitar case. He set it gently on the floor in front of Tyler and flipped open the latches to reveal a stunning new acoustic guitar with Tyler's name imprinted on it.

Tyler's mouth fell open. "Jack... this is incredible. Thank you so much!"

Jack grinned. "I figured you'd need a proper guitar for all the music you'll be playing at home, and when you're on the road someday."

Sue hugged Tyler again as everyone gathered around to admire the guitar and the phone. A few more small gifts appeared gift cards, books, and even a new strap for his guitar from one of the girls in the karate class.

"Sandy, how would you know I could use a guitar strap?" Tyler asked?

She glanced at Jack and said, "oh, a little birdie told me!"

Everyone laughed!

Finally, Tyler's mother stepped forward with a smile, her eyes misty with emotion. "Happy birthday, sweetheart," she said softly, wrapping him in a tight hug. "I'm so proud of you."

Tyler's face flushed with happiness as he looked around at the crowd of friends and family who had gathered just for him. He strummed a few soft chords on his new guitar, then glanced at Sue, his smile growing even wider.

"This is the best birthday ever," he said quietly. "Thank you, everyone."

The room filled with cheers, laughter, and the sound of Tyler's guitar as the pizza was passed around and the celebration continued.

The party was winding down, the last few slices of pizza disappearing from the boxes and the sounds of laughter and music filling the store. Friends lingered, chatting and congratulating Tyler on his gifts. The soft strumming of his new guitar created a gentle background melody as he tested the chords, his smile as wide as the room.

Tyler's mother stepped forward from the small group she had been quietly chatting with. She glanced at the others, her voice gentle but steady.

"Excuse me, everyone," she said, raising her hand slightly. "Could I have your attention for just a moment?"

The room grew quiet as the chatter faded. Tyler glanced up from his guitar, his eyes widening slightly with surprise. "Mom?"

She smiled warmly, though there was a hint of nervousness in her expression. "Tyler, I know the years haven't always been easy for us. Without your father, it has been just the two of us for a long time. And I have worked hard to make sure you have had what you needed, even when things were tough."

A hush fell over the room, the quiet weight of her words settling over everyone. Tyler's cheeks flushed pink, and he set his guitar aside, standing straighter as his mother continued.

"I've saved and planned for this day," she said, her voice growing softer but more confident. She reached into her purse and pulled out a small box, wrapped neatly in silver paper with a simple bow. She stepped closer to her son, holding it out to him. "Happy birthday, son. I love you."

Tyler's hands trembled slightly as he accepted the box, the weight of his mother's words sinking in. Slowly, he unwrapped it, the paper falling away to reveal a small set of car keys nestled inside. His brow furrowed in confusion as he held them up, glancing between the keys and his mother.

"Mom?" he asked, puzzled. "What is this? What car?"

His mother's smile grew brighter, her eyes shimmering with unshed tears. "It's the keys to your new car," she said softly.

Tyler's eyes widened. "My car?"

She nodded, her voice trembling slightly with emotion. "Yes. It is a 2025 Chevy van. I know it is not a sports car, and you would have preferred something flashier. But when I talked to Jack" she glanced briefly at Jack, who nodded in quiet agreement "he told me stories about his days on the road, sleeping in his pickup truck during those long trips for gigs."

Jack's voice rumbled in from behind, full of fond nostalgia. "It was not glamorous, believe me. But it was what I could manage at the time. You will need something more comfortable for when you are traveling, Tyler."

Tyler's mother nodded. "Exactly. I wanted to make sure you would have something reliable and comfortable. Something where you can stretch out, put a mattress in the back, and have a decent place to sleep on your singing tours. It is not just a vehicle it is a home on wheels for the nights when you're chasing your dreams."

The entire room was silent as the meaning of her gift settled in. Tyler's eyes shimmered with tears, and he clutched the keys tightly, his lips trembling. He stepped forward and wrapped his mother in a fierce, tearful hug.

"Mom, it's perfect," he whispered, his voice thick with emotion. "Thank you. Thank you so much."

She hugged him back, her own tears falling freely now. "I'm so proud of you, Tyler. I know you are going to do amazing things. I just wanted to give you a good start."

As they held each other, the room erupted into soft applause, the friends and family gathered there clapping and wiping at their own eyes. Even Sue blinked back tears, her hand resting gently on Tyler's shoulder as he stepped back, wiping his face with the sleeve of his shirt.

Jack stepped closer, his voice full of warmth. "She's right, kid. You are going to go far and having that van will make the road a little easier. Trust me."

Tyler chuckled through his tears, his voice breaking with gratitude. "I cannot believe it. A van. My own van. It's... it is perfect." He looked back at his mother. "And it is so much more than a car. It is a symbol of everything you have done for me, everything you have sacrificed. I will never forget this."

His mother's smile trembled as she reached up to cup his cheek. "That is all I wanted, Tyler. For you to know how much I love you and to believe in yourself as much as I believe in you."

Sue stepped forward then, her voice teasing but gentle. "Looks like you're going to have a hard time topping this birthday, huh?"

Tyler laughed, his cheeks still wet with tears. "Yeah. This is the best birthday ever. I don't think anything could beat it."

Emily grinned. "Well, there's still cupcakes to look forward to," she teased, gesturing toward the small dessert table where a cupcake awaited one with candles ready to be lit.

The group gathered around, lighting the candles and singing a joyful rendition of "Happy Birthday" as Tyler stood in the center, his new guitar by his side, his phone tucked safely into his pocket, and the keys to his future resting firmly in his hand.

As he blew out the candles, the room erupted into cheers, laughter, and applause.

Jack, stepping forward with a grin and clapping Tyler on the back, leaned in and said loud enough for everyone to hear, "Now Tyler, just remember your Christian values when you and Sue are on a date in your van..."

The whole room burst into laughter, with even Tyler covering his face in mock embarrassment as Sue swatted playfully at Jack's arm.

Emily shook her head, giggling. "Oh, Jack."

"Hey, I'm just saying," Jack said, his grin widening. "Better to remind him now than later!"

With laughter echoing through the store, the party continued into the evening, filled with love, music, and a few good-natured jokes making it a birthday Tyler would never forget.

As Tyler took his first bite of the cupcake remembering that Sue made them, he jokingly started a fake choking and cough.

Sue, reached over and slapped Tyler on his arm, "Stop it" Sue said, they are not that bad!"

Tyler looked at Sue, "no, they are actually pretty good!"

Everyone laughed!

# Chapter Ten: Gifts of Love and Gratitude

The house was quiet and peaceful when Emily and Jack finally got home after the party. The scent of leftover pizza clung faintly to their clothes, but neither minded. They were too wrapped up in the warmth of the day, the laughter of friends, and the memory of Tyler's tearful embrace when he had unwrapped the van keys.

Jack dropped onto the couch, pulling Emily down beside him. She tucked her legs under herself, leaning into his side as he wrapped an arm around her. The room was softly lit, the hum of the refrigerator in the background, and for a few long moments, they just sat there, letting the quiet settle around them.

Finally, Emily stirred. "I can't believe how much we got done today," she murmured.

Jack grinned, brushing a strand of hair from her cheek. "Cake, flowers, pizza, and Tyler's best birthday ever."

She smiled, but her mind was already ticking through the list. "But we are not done yet. We still need to figure out the catering for the wedding reception."

Jack nodded, stretching his legs out. "And we have barely even talked about a bachelorette or bachelor party. You know, for the record, I am willing to fund both. I figure it is worth it send you off to your last weekend of freedom in style."

Emily laughed, her head tilting back against his shoulder. "You are ridiculous. But thank you. Just remember no girls at your party!"

Jack laughed, "Who me, girls?"

Emily, "You know Christian values!"

They sat for a few more minutes, talking through the remaining details. Emily grabbed a notepad and pen from the side table, jotting down a list.

"Okay, so we have got:

- Cake: ordered and scheduled.
- Flowers: ordered and scheduled.
- Tuxedos and dresses: ordered and scheduled.
- Tyler's birthday: success.
- Music: we will still need a playlist or band for the reception, unless we produce something better.
- Catering: still open.
- Photographer: I almost forgot.
- Bachelorette and bachelor parties: to plan."

Jack scanned the list, his hand tracing the page absentmindedly. "It is coming together, Em. I know it feels overwhelming, but we have already checked off a lot. This is going to be a wedding people talk about for years."

Emily sighed contentedly. "I hope so. And not just because of how much pizza we have consumed in the planning."

They both laughed, the sound filling the cozy living room.

Jack searched his phone for a local photographer, "heres one Sandra Photography, call anytime!" Jack pressed call and on the fourth ring, "sandra photography how can I help you?" Jack introduced himself talked about the wedding and the deal was set. Cross off another line.

Just as they were winding down, Jack's phone buzzed loudly on the coffee table, breaking the quiet. They both jumped slightly, exchanging a surprised glance.

Jack reached for the phone, squinting at the screen. "It's Bethany from Nashville," he said, a bit surprised. "Wonder what she's calling about this late."

He answered. "Hey, Bethany. How are you?"

Her voice came through the line, warm and enthusiastic. "Jack! I just wanted to check in with you about the recording. Are you still good for the studio dates we talked about?"

Jack leaned forward, balancing the phone between his ear and shoulder. "Yes, I'm still good. I just had to get through a few things here first. But I'm ready to go when the time comes, Monday the 18th!"

Bethany chuckled softly. "Good to hear. And congratulations on the engagement. I heard through the grapevine about the wedding."

Jack's smile widened. "Thanks, Bethany. We are excited. It is coming together a little faster than we expected, but it is going to be great. It is a week from Saturday!"

Bethany's voice turned thoughtful. "Well, I do not want you worrying too much about the reception entertainment. As my gift to you and Emily, I will handle the music and entertainment. I will take care of everything. Just focus on getting married and enjoying the day."

Jack's eyebrows lifted, stunned. "Bethany... that is incredibly generous. You do not have to do that."

"I want to," she insisted. "Consider it my wedding gift to you both. You have always been there for others, Jack. Let me be there for you now."

Jack's voice softened. "Thank you. That means more than I can say."

They chatted for a few more minutes, confirming the recording schedule and touching base on the wedding date. When they finally hung up, Jack leaned back against the couch, his head resting against the cushion.

"Well," he said with a laugh, turning to Emily, "there's one thing off our list. Bethany's handling the entertainment."

Emily's eyes widened in surprise. "Really? That's amazing! I was starting to think we would have to hire a local band or just use a playlist."

Jack grinned. "Not anymore. She has got it covered."

Before they could settle back into the couch, Emily's phone rang. She picked it up, seeing the pastor's name on the screen. "It's Pastor Raymin," she said, answering with a curious smile. "Hi, Pastor. How are you?"

His warm, familiar voice greeted her. "Hi, Emily. I just wanted to check if you have finished the catering for the wedding yet."

Emily laughed softly. "No, not yet. We have been so busy with everything else today, I have not had a chance to call any caterers."

"That's actually perfect," the pastor said, his tone brightening and coughing. "Because my wife and the ladies of the church have been talking, and we would love to cater your wedding as our gift to you and Jack. You two have done so much for this community, and we want to give back. Please, let us handle it."

Emily's mouth fell open in surprise. "Pastor... that is so generous. You really do not have to do that, why have you not kicked that cold yet, you should see a doctor I mean it!"

He chuckled softly. "I will consider it, anyway we want to. Consider it a small way to show our love and appreciation. You and Jack have given so much of yourselves to this community. You have sown kindness and service, and now it is coming back to you. You reap what you sow, Emily. This is just a little harvest of gratitude."

Tears pricked Emily's eyes as she covered her mouth with her hand. "Thank you, Pastor. I... we really appreciate it. Please tell your wife and the ladies thank you from both of us."

When she hung up, she turned to Jack, her voice trembling with emotion. "The pastor and the church ladies are catering the wedding for us. As their gift."

Jack's eyes widened in astonishment. "Wow. That is incredible."

"They said we've done so much for the community, it's just their way of giving back," Emily murmured. "He said... 'You reap what you sow.'" He still sounds terrible, I hope he sees a doctor!"

Jack leaned closer, brushing a tear from her cheek. "Well, I'd say we've planted some pretty good seeds along the way."

Emily laughed softly, resting her head against his shoulder. "We're really blessed, aren't we?"

Jack nodded, wrapping his arm around her. "Yeah, we are. And it is not just about what we have done it is about who we have become together. This community, our friends, our family they are part of us. And I cannot wait to marry you and keep building this life." "I love you, Jack!" "I love you too Em!" They kissed.

They sat there in the quiet, the weight of the day's events sinking in, the to-do list on the notepad now finished no longer feeling so daunting. With love, laughter, and the support of their community surrounding them, they knew that everything would come together just as it always had.

They sat together on the couch, the quiet hum of the house surrounding them. Emily sighed, leaning back against Jack's chest, her fingers lightly tracing the notepad resting on her lap.

"I hope the pastor isn't getting sick," she said softly, her brow furrowed. "He coughed a few times on the phone. It didn't sound too bad, but..."

Jack chuckled lightly. "That would be all we need, huh? The pastor coming down with something and not being able to marry us."

Emily swatted his arm playfully, sitting up straighter. "Do not say that, Jack! If the pastor could not do it, we would be in trouble. I would not be able to stay in the same hotel room with you until we are married!"

Jack laughed, pulling her back against him. "That is true. We would have to get creative."

Emily rolled her eyes but could not help laughing with him. "You are terrible. But seriously I hope he is fine. I will call him in a couple of days and check in. Maybe bring him and his wife some soup or something. We need him healthy and ready for the wedding."

Jack kissed her temple, his voice low and teasing. "And you need me in that hotel room, huh?"

Emily groaned, hiding her face against his shoulder. "You're impossible."

But the laughter that filled the room was light and genuine, wrapping around them like a comforting blanket. They both knew that no matter what challenges came their way from coughing pastors to wedding plans their love and the community surrounding them would see them through.

# Chapter Eleven: Party Plans and Music Nights

The next morning dawned with a sense of renewed energy. Emily stood in the record store with Sue, both sipping coffees as they chatted between customers. The buzz of conversation from the few patrons was a soft backdrop to their discussion.

"I was thinking," Emily said thoughtfully, swirling her coffee in its cup. "We should plan a small bachelorette party. Nothing wild just something fun with some of the ladies from church. Jack said he would cover the costs. And of course, Mary should come too."

Sue's eyes brightened as she leaned against the counter. "That sounds like a great idea. Something low-key and meaningful, right? What do you have in mind?"

"Exactly," Emily nodded. "Just a small gathering. Maybe a few games, some snacks, and a little time to relax before the wedding chaos really ramps up."

Sue considered for a moment, then grinned. "How about my place? We could do it Sunday afternoon after church. That way everyone can come without disrupting family plans, and it will be casual."

Emily's face lit up with gratitude. "That's perfect, Sue. Thank you. I will call a few of the ladies today and invite them. Nothing big just a chance to connect and enjoy some time together."

Sue's voice was light with a hint of mischief. "And of course, we will make sure it is a surprise for you, even if you are the bride. You deserve a little bit of pampering."

Emily laughed, her cheeks flushing. "You are terrible. But thank you. It means a lot to me to have this support."

Meanwhile, on the other side of town, Jack parked his truck outside Tyler's house after school and climbed the steps to the front door.

He knocked, waiting only a moment before Tyler appeared, a curious expression on his face.

"Hey, Jack," Tyler said, stepping aside to let him in. "What's up?"

Jack clapped him on the shoulder as they moved into the living room. "I wanted to talk to you about your bachelor party. You know, its tradition, but I figured you have not thought much about it."

Tyler's brows furrowed. "Bachelor party? I have not even thought about it. I thought those were just for guys who want wild nights and lap dances or something."

Jack chuckled. "That's one version, yeah. But I was thinking we would do something different. Something that feels like you. Some drinks, light sandwiches, chips. A nice, clean party. We can invite the pastor and your gang from church. You could even bring your new guitar, and we will sing a few songs together. Doesn't have to be anything crazy."

Tyler relaxed, a smile forming. "That sounds a lot better than I imagined. I am not into anything wild, and honestly, I would rather have a night where we can all just enjoy each other's company. When were you thinking?"

Jack thought for a moment. "The wedding's a week from Saturday, so how about Saturday evening? It is short notice, but we can make it happen. Just a few days away, but nothing fancy just a fun time with good people."

Tyler nodded enthusiastically. "That sounds great. I can handle that. I will bring my new guitar, and we can all hang out. Thanks for making it something comfortable for me, Jack."

Jack grinned. "Of course. It's my night, Tyler. And trust me, it will be a good one."

Back at the record store, Emily was still discussing the bachelorette party details with Sue and Mary. "So, Sunday afternoon works for everyone?" Emily asked, jotting down notes on a small notepad. They made phone calls throughout the afternoon and everyone they called agreed to come to the party.

Mary nodded, her excitement clear. "That is perfect. I can help you set up and clean up, Sue."

Sue grinned. "Thanks, Mary. We will make it a nice afternoon. We can have some finger foods, a little dessert, and a few party games to keep it fun. Emily deserves a break from all this planning."

Emily laughed softly. "You are spoiling me. But I will take it. Just something simple where we can relax, share stories, and pray together for the wedding. That sounds like heaven right now."

Sue leaned closer. "Speaking of the wedding, have you decided on any last-minute details? Decorations, the ceremony script, anything like that?"

Emily sighed, her smile tinged with a hint of nervousness. "We have covered most of it, but there are always trivial things popping up. The decorations are almost done, the pastor has our vows, and the catering is covered thanks to the church ladies. Bethany's handling the entertainment for the reception. It is really coming together, but my head's still spinning."

Mary chimed in, her tone warm and reassuring. "It is going to be a beautiful day, Emily. Everything is falling into place, and you have got so many people who love you and Jack. It is all going to be perfect."

Emily's eyes shimmered with gratitude as she reached over to squeeze Mary's hand. "Thank you, Mary. That means so much to me."

The rest of the afternoon passed in a blur of phone calls, customer interactions, and shared laughter. As 3 o'clock approached, Emily stepped outside to catch a few moments of fresh air. Jack's truck pulled into the parking lot, and he hopped out, his face bright with news.

"Hey, ladies," he called as he entered the store. "I just talked to Tyler. We are setting up his bachelor party for Saturday evening. Drinks, light snacks, and some music. It is going to be an enjoyable time."

Sue grinned. "Sounds like you have gotten it all planned out. Nothing too crazy, right, no girls?"

Jack laughed. "Nope. Just a nice, clean party with friends and family. Pastor's coming, and Tyler's bringing his new guitar. Should be an enjoyable way to relax."

Emily smiled, relief washing over her. "That is perfect. And we have the bachelorette party at Sue's place on Sunday. Everything is coming together."

Jack leaned in and kissed her cheek. "See? I told you we'd figure it out. And just think in a week, we will be husband and wife."

Emily's cheeks flushed pink as she wrapped her arms around him. "I can't wait."

As they stood there, surrounded by the familiar walls of the record store and the gentle hum of music in the background, it was clear that while the wedding day would be the culmination of their journey, these moments the laughter, the planning, the community coming together were the true heart of their story.

And as Jack, Emily, Sue, and Mary prepared for a weekend of simple, heartfelt celebrations, they knew that their love, grounded in faith and friendship, would carry them through every challenge, every joy, and every shared song.

# Chapter Eleven: The Parties Begin

Saturday evening arrived with a gentle breeze rustling the trees outside Emily and Jack's home. The house had been prepped earlier in the day, with tables set up in the living room and kitchen, a selection of light snacks arranged on platters, and cold drinks chilling in the fridge.

Jack glanced around with satisfaction. "We are set. Chips, sandwiches, drinks... and Tyler's bringing his new guitar."

Emily stood at the doorway, smoothing her dress. "It is going to be great. And Sue and I will be out of your hair we are going to catch a movie and let you all have the house for the evening."

Sue chimed in with a grin as she stepped inside. "We will leave before the guys show up, and we will make it back before things wind down. Just enough time for us to enjoy our own little outing."

Jack gave them both a thumbs-up. "Perfect. You girls enjoy yourselves, and we will keep things tame here."

Just as Emily grabbed her purse and Sue was about to follow, Emily's phone buzzed. She glanced at the screen and her heart skipped. "It's Pastor Raymin," she said softly. She quickly answered. "Hello, Pastor?"

His voice on the other end was warm but tinged with exhaustion. "Hi, Emily. I just wanted to let you know I am at the hospital. I have not been feeling well all day. I had a headache, chills, and a cough, and then my breathing got a little tight. They tested me for COVID, and I will get the results soon. They are keeping me overnight for observation."

Emily's breath caught, her heart sinking. "Oh no, Pastor. I am so sorry. How are you feeling now?"

"Tired," he admitted, his voice low. "They are taking good care of me, but I will not be able to handle the service tomorrow. I did not want you to worry about the church. I spoke with Reverend Ottman he has agreed to step in for me. He is retired but more than willing to help."

Relief mingled with concern as Emily nodded, though he could not see it. "Thank you for letting us know. Please, focus on resting and getting better. We will keep you in our prayers, and I will check in with your wife tomorrow."

"Thank you, Emily. And do not worry your wedding will be in good hands. If I cannot officiate, I will make sure someone else can step in. Now go enjoy your evening. You deserve it."

After they hung up, Emily relayed the news to Jack and Sue. Her voice was soft, but she tried to stay upbeat. "Pastors in the hospital. He is showing COVID symptoms headache, chills, cough, some breathing issues. They are keeping him overnight. Reverend Ottman, the pastor, who was here before Pastor Raymin, is stepping in for church service tomorrow."

Jack rubbed the back of his neck, his brow furrowing. "That is rough. I hope he is going to be okay. It sounds like it could be COVID."

Sue shook her head, her expression sympathetic. "We will all pray for him. And it is good that Reverend Ottman is stepping in. At least the church is covered, and the congregation will not be left wondering what is happening."

Emily nodded, her smile faint but grateful. "I am glad he thought ahead. Now, let us focus on what we can control Jack, you enjoy your guys' night here. Sue and I will go relax at the movies. We will check on Pastor in the morning."

As the clock ticked closer to the party's start time, Emily and Sue gathered their things and left, leaving Jack to greet the guys as they arrived.

Not long after, Tyler showed up with his guitar case in hand, a wide smile lighting up his face. His friends from church arrived next, followed by a few familiar faces from his karate group. Jack welcomed them in, offering drinks and snacks as they settled into the living room.

"Glad you all could make it," Jack said as he clapped Tyler on the shoulder. "Let us keep it simple good company, some music, and a few laughs. No crazy bachelor party stuff tonight."

Tyler grinned. "That sounds perfect. Thanks, Jack."

The group gathered around, passing plates of sandwiches and bowls of chips. The air was filled with easy conversation and the soft strumming of Tyler's guitar as he played familiar songs, his voice blending with Jack's on a few harmonies.

Meanwhile, at the theater, Emily and Sue settled into their seats with popcorn and soda in hand. Sue nudged Emily playfully. "You know, for a bachelorette party, this is pretty chill."

Emily laughed softly. "Exactly how I like it. After everything this week, I just needed a quiet night with a good movie and a great friend."

Sue's smile widened. "We will make up for it tomorrow at my place. Just us girls, some finger food, and lots of laughs. I will even plan a few surprise games."

Emily sighed with contentment. "That sounds perfect. And we will keep praying Pastor gets better soon."

The night passed with quiet joy on both fronts' music, laughter, and friendship for the guys at Emily's house, and a comforting movie night for the ladies. Despite the concern hanging over them, they each found a moment of peace and connection.

As the credits rolled at the theater, Sue glanced at Emily. "Ready to head back?"

Emily nodded. "Let us go check in on the guys. Hopefully, Jack has not turned the living room into a concert hall."

They left the theater, stepping into the cool night air, their hearts light with hope for the days ahead.

Sunday morning arrived with soft golden sunlight filtering through the curtains. Emily awoke with a heavy heart, knowing today would confirm what everyone in town had feared since the first whispers of Pastor Raymin's illness. She went downstairs.

"You're up early," Jack murmured, his voice still rough with sleep.

Emily sighed, turning to face him. "I just have this feeling today is going to be tough. I am worried about Pastor."

Jack pressed a gentle kiss to her forehead. "We will get through it. The church will too. Come on, let us get ready. We will stand together."

By the time they pulled into the church parking lot, Tyler and Sue were already there, waiting near the entrance. Sue gave Emily a quick, comforting hug. "It's going to be okay. We will pray together."

Inside, the church felt unusually subdued. The familiar rustle of hymnals and whispered greetings were absent; instead, the congregation sat in quiet anticipation. Reverend Ottman, a tall man with a kind, weathered face, stood at the pulpit, his expression solemn but resolute.

When everyone had settled, he cleared his throat, his voice echoing through the sanctuary. "Brothers and sisters, I bring news this morning that weighs heavily on our hearts. Our beloved Pastor Raymin has tested positive for COVID. He is currently under care at the hospital, and while his condition is stable, he is still in need of our prayers and support. This morning, I ask that we join as one family of faith, lifting him and his family to the Lord."

A wave of murmured concern rippled through the congregation. Sue reached over to squeeze Emily's hand, and Tyler bowed his head, his brow furrowed with worry. Jack sat upright, his arm wrapped protectively around Emily's shoulders.

Reverend Ottman raised his hands, and the church fell into a reverent hush. "Let us pray."

The sanctuary became a haven of shared faith as Reverend Ottman led them in a heartfelt prayer, his voice trembling with emotion but unwavering in conviction. He prayed for Pastor Raymin's swift and complete recovery, for the comfort of his family, for strength and protection over the congregation, and for guidance for the days to come.

His words flowed with sincerity and love, weaving through the quiet space like a warm embrace: "Heavenly Father, we come to You this morning with heavy hearts, lifting our brother, Pastor Raymin, into Your hands. We ask that You grant him strength in his body, peace in his mind, and comfort in his spirit. Be with the doctors and nurses caring for him; grant them wisdom and steady hands. Surround his family with Your presence and remind them that they are not alone. And Lord, as a church family, bind us together in love, that we may support one another through this trial and appear stronger in faith and unity. In Jesus' name, we pray. Amen."

As the prayer concluded, the congregation remained silent for a moment, each person reflecting on the pastor's impact on their lives. Reverend Ottman then continued, "Let us now join our voices together in the prayer our Savior taught us."

With one voice, the entire church recited the Lord's Prayer, their words rising in a powerful chorus:

"Our Father, who art in heaven,
Hallowed be Thy name.
Thy kingdom come,
Thy will be done,
On earth as it is in heaven.
Give us this day our daily bread,
And forgive us our trespasses,
As we forgive those who trespass against us.
And lead us not into temptation,
But deliver us from evil.
For Thine is the kingdom, and the power, and the glory, forever. Amen."

The prayer echoed through the church, weaving its way through every heart, offering comfort and unity in a moment of shared vulnerability. As the final "Amen" was spoken, the congregation sat back in their pews, some wiping away tears, others clasping hands in silent solidarity.

Reverend Ottman delivered a short but poignant sermon about the power of community, reminding them that even in times of uncertainty, faith binds them together. His words were simple, heartfelt, and exactly what they needed to hear.

When the service concluded, people lingered, exchanging quiet words of support and comfort. Emily, Jack, Sue, and Tyler gathered near the front, talking softly about the service and sharing prayers for the pastor's recovery.

Just then, the mayor approached, his polished shoes tapping softly against the wooden floor. He was a tall man with a reassuring presence and a warm smile, dressed in a well-fitted navy suit. He greeted them with a nod. "Emily, Jack," he said, extending his hand. "It's good to see you both this morning."

Emily and Jack turned to him, surprised but grateful for his presence. "Good morning, Mayor," Emily said, her voice tinged with emotion. "Thank you for being here today."

The mayor's expression softened. "I wanted to speak with you both. I heard about Pastor Raymin's illness, and I know how much he means to you and to this church. I want you to know that under the laws of this state, as mayor, I have the authority to officiate weddings. It would be my honor to step in and marry you if Pastor Raymin is not well enough to do so."

For a moment, Emily and Jack were too stunned to respond. Emily's eyes shimmered with gratitude as she glanced at Jack, her hand tightening around his. Jack returned her look, his smile full of warmth and quiet strength.

"That would be wonderful," Emily said softly, her voice steady despite the emotions swirling in her chest.

Jack nodded. "Yes, Mayor, we would be honored. Thank you for offering."

The mayor's smile brightened. "It is settled, then. I will speak with Pastor Raymin to make the arrangements and ensure everything is handled smoothly. Let us plan to meet here at the church Thursday evening for a quick rehearsal. Afterward, I would love to take you all out for dinner my treat. Think of it as my wedding gift to you."

Emily's heart lifted, the weight of uncertainty easing from her shoulders. "Thank you, Mayor. That is incredibly kind of you."

Jack shook the mayor's hand firmly. "We genuinely appreciate it. This community has shown us so much love and support."

Sue, standing nearby, added with a grin, "It is amazing how everyone is stepping up. We are blessed to have such a strong community around us."

The mayor nodded. "That is what makes Pineville special. We take care of each other. And do not worry I will make sure your wedding is perfect."

As he stepped away to speak with other members of the congregation, Emily turned to Jack, her eyes shining. "I did not expect this. Everyone is helping, and now even the mayor is stepping in. It is overwhelming, but in an enjoyable way."

Jack wrapped his arm around her. "That is the beauty of this town. When one of us needs help, everyone comes together. And you know what they say you reap what you sow."

Emily smiled, leaning into his embrace. "I guess we've been sowing good seeds all along."

Sue and Tyler joined them, the sun streaming through the church doors as they stepped into the fresh air. The day felt a little brighter, the future a little clearer, and their hearts a little lighter knowing that, no matter what challenges lay ahead, they had each other and a whole community standing with them.

That afternoon, Sue's cozy house buzzed with laughter and conversation as Emily's closest friends gathered to celebrate her upcoming wedding. The party started at 1:30, just like the guys' gathering, with a spread of finger sandwiches, chips, bowls of mixed nuts, and colorful platters of fresh fruit and veggies. Sparkling lemonade and a few chilled bottles of wine added a festive touch.

Sue had set up a long table in her dining room, covered with a white tablecloth and decorated with pink and peach streamers. In one corner stood a stack of wrapped presents, each adorned with ribbons and tags bearing familiar names from Emily's circle of friends.

As the ladies mingled, laughing and sharing stories, Sue clinked her glass to get everyone's attention. "All right, ladies, it is time to spoil our bride-to-be! Emily, take the seat of honor. Let us see what treasures we have all brought you!"

Emily blushed but smiled as she sat down, her heart full of gratitude for the love surrounding her. One by one, the women handed her gifts, each thoughtfully chosen and filled with excitement for her new life with Jack.

Here is a peek at the gifts Emily unwrapped:

Sue's Gift: Sue grinned mischievously as Emily tore into the tissue paper to reveal a silky, peach-colored lingerie set a delicate lace chemise with a matching robe. "Something a little daring for the honeymoon," Sue teased, making everyone laugh.

Mary's Gift: Mary's package was wrapped neatly in silver paper, having a personalized leather-bound prayer journal embossed with Emily's initials. Inside, Mary had written a heartfelt message of blessings for Emily and Jack's marriage.

Laura's Gift: Laura, a friend from Emily's Bible study group, gave her a kitchen essentials basket filled with pretty dish towels, a monogrammed cutting board, and a set of wooden spoons. "For all the home-cooked meals you'll share," she said warmly.

Rachel's Gift: Rachel, an old friend from high school, presented Emily with a spa gift set a collection of bath bombs, luxurious lotions, and scented candles. "You'll need this to relax after all the wedding stress," Rachel joked, making the group giggle.

Jenna's Gift: Jenna, a newer friend from church, gave Emily a recipe book for newlyweds, with a handwritten note inside suggesting a double-date dinner at their favorite local diner once Emily and Jack settled into married life.

Sue's Mom's Gift: Sue's mother, who had always treated Emily like one of her own, handed her a beautifully wrapped box containing a keepsake pearl necklace and earrings. "For something classic and elegant on your wedding day," she said, her voice touched with emotion.

As Emily unwrapped each gift, her cheeks flushed pink with happiness and surprise. The laughter, stories, and playful teasing made the afternoon fly by, each gift a reminder of the love and support surrounding her.

When the last package was opened and the last glass of lemonade poured, Emily stood, wiping a happy tear from her cheek. "Thank you all so much. I do not even have words. This means everything to me. I am so blessed to have each of you in my life. I cannot wait to celebrate with all of you at the wedding."

The women raised their glasses in a toast. "To Emily!" they cheered.

"To love, laughter, and happily ever after," Sue added with a wink.

As the party wound down and the sun dipped lower in the sky, Emily felt her heart swell with gratitude. The community's love, her friends' laughter, and the promises of the future shimmered around her like a blessing she could carry into her new life.

# Chapter Twelve: A Night to Remember

As the bachelorette party wound down at Sue's cozy house, the laughter and the last crumbs of sandwiches filled the air. Emily was glowing with happiness, surrounded by her friends and the thoughtful gifts they had showered her with. The sun outside was beginning its slow descent, casting long golden rays through the windows. The day felt complete, a day filled with love, laughter, and anticipation for the coming wedding.

Sue's phone buzzed just as she was walking Emily to the door, where Jack was waiting to take her home. Sue glanced down at the screen and felt her heart flutter it was Tyler.

She quickly answered. "Hey, Tyler! What's up?"

His voice, warm and easy, flowed through the line. "Hey, beautiful. How about we make the evening even better? Would you like to go for a ride in my van?"

Sue felt her cheeks flush, a grin spreading across her face. "That sounds amazing."

"I'll be there in twenty," Tyler said. "I have something to show you."

Sue's heart skipped a beat as she ended the call and turned back to the women still tidying up from the party. "Sorry, girls, but I have plans," she said with a playful grin. "Tyler's picking me up."

The girls laughed and teased her, but Sue was already pulling her jacket on, her heart fluttering in anticipation.

Mary said, "go have fun Sue, I will finish cleaning this up."

Sue, "Thank you so much!" They hugged.

Twenty minutes later, right on time, the familiar rumble of Tyler's van echoed in her driveway. Sue stepped outside, her breath catching as she saw him leaning casually against the driver's door, a confident yet shy smile lighting his face.

"Hey," she said, her voice soft.

"Hey yourself," Tyler replied, pushing off the van and holding the door open for her. "Ready for a little adventure?"

She climbed in, her eyes widening as she glanced around. "Tyler... what is this?"

The back of the van had been transformed into a cozy retreat. He had installed a plush love seat that could fold out into a queen bed, with soft throw blankets and a couple of large pillows. A small flat-screen TV was mounted on the side, connected to a portable movie player. Fairy lights lined the edges, casting a soft, romantic glow.

Tyler rubbed the back of his neck, suddenly a little shy. "I thought it might be fun. You know, for long trips or just to have a space for us to hang out."

Sue's eyes sparkled. "It is perfect. Can we go somewhere and watch a movie?"

"I was hoping you'd say that" Tyler grinned. "How about the park? We can pick up some pizza and soda on the way."

Sue's stomach growled softly at the mention of food, and she laughed. "That sounds amazing."

They stopped at a local pizzeria, picking up a large pepperoni pizza and a couple of bottles of root beer. The scent of warm, cheesy goodness filled the van as they drove toward the park, the sun dipping lower into the horizon. By the time they reached a quiet spot by the lake, dusk had fallen, painting the sky in shades of lavender and rose.

Tyler parked, turned off the engine, and flipped on the fairy lights. He opened the pizza box between them and set up the movie "A Walk to Remember" on the screen.

As the familiar opening chords of the movie played, Sue nestled against Tyler on the love seat, a slice of pizza in hand. They laughed quietly over the clinking of soda bottles and the rustle of the pizza box, sharing bites and the comfort of each other's presence.

The movie's gentle, emotional story unfolded, pulling them into its world of love, faith, and transformation. Sue felt tears prick at her eyes during the tender moments, while Tyler brushed a kiss against her temple, his own heart swelling with the emotions onscreen and the feeling of Sue in his arms.

As the night deepened and the air grew colder, Sue shivered slightly. Without a word, Tyler reached behind the love seat and pulled out a thick, soft blanket. He wrapped it around them both, pulling her closer into his side.

"Better?" he murmured.

Sue nodded, snuggling closer, her head resting against his chest as they watched the movie's ending. The characters' declarations of love mirrored the unspoken feelings stirring between them, and the soft glow of the fairy lights made the moment feel timeless.

When the credits rolled and the last strains of music faded, they sat in silence for a few minutes, the sounds of nature outside blending with the quiet beating of their hearts.

"I'm glad you called," Sue whispered.

Tyler tightened his arm around her. "I needed to see you tonight. You make everything feel better, Sue."

Her heart fluttered at his words, and she tilted her face up to his, their eyes meeting in the soft light. The unspoken question lingered between them, and Tyler's lips brushed hers in a tentative, gentle kiss.

As they parted, Sue's breath caught, her cheeks warming. But Tyler was not finished. His lips found hers again, this time with more confidence, a few lingering kisses followed by shorter, playful ones. They both laughed softly, the van now filled with shared breath and whispered promises.

"I love you," Tyler murmured against her lips.

Sue's eyes shimmered with emotion. "I love you, too."

They sat there, wrapped in each other's arms, the night wrapping around them like a blessing. Eventually, as the moon rose high in the sky and the air turned crisp, Tyler started the engine and drove her home, the silence between them filled with contentment and the quiet echo of a night well spent.

When they reached her house, Tyler shifted the van into park and turned to her, his face serious but gentle. "Sue," he said softly, "would it be okay if I gave you a kiss goodnight?"

Her heart swelled at the sweetness of his request. "Yes," she whispered.

Their kiss was tender and lingering, a perfect blend of shy and bold, of new love and deepening connection. A few long kisses melted into several shorter ones, each one a promise of more to come. When they finally parted, both were breathless and a little giddy.

"I love you," Tyler said softly, his forehead resting against hers.

"I love you, too," Sue replied, her smile radiant.

As she stepped out of the van and turned to wave goodnight, Tyler watched her with a heart so full he thought it might burst. He waited until she was safely inside before driving away, the memory of their night together etched into his heart forever.

# Chapter Thirteen: The Last Karate Class for Jack

The warm glow of late afternoon sun streamed through the tall windows of Pineville Community Church's fellowship hall. The floor gleamed from a fresh polish, the scent of lemon cleaner faint beneath the rustle of sneakers and quiet conversation. Today was no ordinary class it was the final karate session before the wedding, and everyone had gathered with an air of anticipation and camaraderie.

Jack stood at the front, his familiar presence steadying the room. His black belt was tied neatly at his waist, and his confident smile eased the nervous energy of the assembled group. "All right, everyone," he said, his voice carrying through the hall. "Before we get started, I want to introduce someone special."

He gestured to a tall, broad-shouldered man standing beside him. The man's warm smile and steady gaze commanded attention. His black belt was crisp, his presence radiating quiet strength.

"This is Jim Donahue," Jack continued. "A good friend of mine, fellow black belt, and a lay servant at his church. Since Pastor Raymin is still recovering, Jim's going to handle today's class. And he will be here each Wednesday in my absence. He has also agreed to lead us in prayer."

Jim raised a hand in greeting. "It is great to be here. Jacks told me about this group sounds like you have all been working hard. Let us make this a good session."

A few murmured greetings followed as the class settled into a loose circle. Sue, standing beside Tyler, glanced around and smiled at the familiar faces. Tyler's gang eight of his friends, their faces a mix of excitement and uncertainty had come along, standing slightly apart but eager to be included.

Tyler turned to them with a grin. "Guys, this is Jim. He is legit, and today we are learning from the best."

Jim's eyes swept over the group, his smile widening. "Why don't we go around and introduce ourselves? It is good to know who we are training and praying with today."

One by one, the group spoke:

Officer Bob, tall and fit, offered a quick nod. "Bob Anderson, Pineville PD. Been here since the first session. Always something new to learn."

Officer Mike, a broad-shouldered man with a quick smile. "Mike Hanson. Officer, Pineville PD. Excited to keep up with you all."

Officer Aaron, younger but equally confident, added, "Aaron Phillips. Officer. Glad to be here and ready for a challenge."

Kara, her ponytail bouncing as she grinned. "Kara Thompson. Been coming since the classes started. Love the feeling of getting stronger."

Maddie, standing next to her sister, chimed in. "Maddie Thompson. Learning with my sister and having a blast doing it."

Rachel, offering a shy smile. "Rachel Collins. Here for strength and friendship. This class has been a lifesaver."

Sue, standing a bit closer to Tyler now, smiled brightly. "Sue Miller. New to this but learning fast and loving it."

Tyler, his voice strong and warm. "Tyler Benson. Grateful for what this class has taught me and for the people I have met along the way."

Emily, standing near Jack, her face glowing. "Emily. Just Emily," she said with a laugh. "I'm here for support, strength, and to share this journey with everyone."

Finally, the eight young men from Tyler's gang stepped forward, one by one, each with a mix of nerves and excitement.

Chris, tall with a confident grin. "Chris Mason. Thanks for letting me join today."

Jayden, quiet but resolute. "Jayden Brooks. Glad to be here."

Leo, his hands tucked into his pockets. "Leo Garcia. This is new for me, but I am ready."

Marcus, with an easy smile. "Marcus Lee. Looking forward to learning something today."

Eli, shifting from foot to foot. "Eli Bennett. Hoping I do not embarrass myself."

Damien, his voice low but sincere. "Damien Cruz. Here to support Tyler and learn a few moves."

Omar, his stance relaxed. "Omar Harris. Let us see what this is all about."

Zane, nodding with a grin. "Zane Cooper. Excited to try this."

Jim clapped his hands lightly. "Great introductions. It's clear this is more than just a class it is a family. Before we start, let us pray together, lifting up Pastor Raymin, Jack, and Emily's upcoming wedding, and each other."

He bowed his head, and the group followed, a hush settling over the hall.

"Lord, we come before You today, grateful for this community and the bonds we have built through discipline and faith. We lift up Pastor Raymin grant him healing, strength, and peace. Bless Jack and Emily as they prepare to unite in marriage; may their love be a beacon to others. For each person here today, grant courage, patience, and the determination to grow stronger in body, mind, and spirit. Watch over this town, these families, and this gathering of friends. In Jesus' name, amen."

"Amen," echoed softly around the room, voices blending in reverence.

With the prayer concluded, Jim clapped his hands once more. "All right let's warm up!"

The class divided into pairs, laughter and focus blending as they ran through drills. Officer Bob partnered with Officer Mike, their friendly rivalry evident as they exchanged light jabs and playful grins. Officer Aaron worked with Leo, offering quick corrections and encouragement.

Kara and Maddie practiced their kicks and blocks, their movements sharp and focused, while Rachel and Sue teamed up, laughing as they helped each other perfect stances. Tyler paired up with Chris, his oldest friend, showing blocks and counters with growing confidence.

Jack moved through the room, offering quiet pointers and praise, while Emily stood back, watching with pride.

"You're doing great, guys," Jim called out, moving from pair to pair. "Keep those stances strong. Focus on your breathing. Remember discipline is key."

As the class progressed, a comfortable rhythm settled in. The newcomers, including some of Tyler's gang, gradually loosened up, following the more experienced students and laughing at their own mistakes. Jim's easygoing manner put them at ease, while his skill kept them attentive.

"Nice work, Kara. Maddie, your blocks are improving. Officer Mike, great form. Emily, you have a natural balance. Sue, love the confidence. Tyler, keep those hands up. Chris, you have good instincts. Everyone is doing fantastic," Jim encouraged, his voice filling the space.

The fellowship hall echoed with the sounds of focused movement, punctuated by bursts of laughter and the occasional mock complaint about sore muscles. Tyler's gang, initially hesitant, were now grinning and sharing tips among themselves.

As the session neared its end, Jim gathered everyone into a circle. The group, flushed and breathing hard but smiling, stood shoulder to shoulder.

"I'm proud of you all," Jim said, his tone warm and genuine. "You have built more than skills you have built a community. Remember, it is not about being perfect. It is about showing up, giving your best, and supporting each other. Carry that spirit into your daily lives." Jack stepped forward, his smile wide. "Thanks, Jim. And thank you, everyone, for making these classes so meaningful. This is not goodbye it is just a pause. After the wedding, and Nashville we will pick up where Jim leaves off. Until then, keep practicing, keep growing, and keep supporting each other."

The group clapped, the sound reverberating with energy and gratitude. As they gathered their belongings, hugs and high-fives were exchanged. Plans were made to meet at the wedding, and promises were whispered to keep practicing.

Tyler helped Sue gather her things, their hands brushing and lingering just a bit longer. Emily stood with Jack, her heart full of pride and hope as she watched the connections that had blossomed in the class.

Outside, the sun dipped low, casting long shadows across the parking lot. The bonds of friendship, faith, and community had never felt stronger.

# Chapter Fourteen: The Rehearsal and Dinner

Thursday evening arrived in Pineville with a gentle breeze and a glow of golden light filtering through the church's tall windows. Emily's heart fluttered as she stood at the entrance of the sanctuary with Jack by her side. Sue, Tyler, and Emily's parents, Randy, and Debbie, gathered nearby, their steps light with anticipation.

At the front of the sanctuary stood Mayor Daniel Hutchison, dressed sharply in a navy suit, his presence confident yet approachable. His voice rang clear as he greeted them, "Welcome, everyone. Let us walk through the wedding so you all feel comfortable and confident for Saturday. I have spoken with Pastor Raymin and will honor his usual format, though we will keep things simple and meaningful."

Emily glanced at Jack, her fingers brushing his, comforted by his warm smile. Though Pastor Raymin's absence saddened her, she was grateful for the mayor's willingness to step in.

"Emily," Mayor Hutchison continued, "you will enter through the main doors on your father's arm. Randy, when you reach the front, I will ask, 'Who gives this woman to be married to this man?' You will answer, 'Her mother and I do,' then step aside so Emily can take her place."

Randy, tall and sturdy despite his gruff expression, nodded as he gave Emily a small, reassuring smile. Beside him, Debbie, with her gentle demeanor and twinkling eyes, squeezed Emily's hand.

"Jack," the mayor said, "you will be waiting here with me, positioned to the right. Sue, you will stand beside Emily once she arrives, and Tyler, you will stand next to Jack. We will walk through the steps, and I will show you where to stand."

They rehearsed the entrance, Emily holding tightly to her father's arm. Her heart raced as they approached the front, Jack's gaze steady on her. When they reached the designated spot, Randy's voice was quiet but clear when asked. "Who gives this bride away?" "Her mother and I do."

As he stepped aside, Emily felt a rush of emotion. Debbie's eyes shimmered with pride, and Sue gave her an encouraging nod.

The mayor smiled. "Excellent. Once everyone is in place, I will welcome the guests, share a few words, and go ahead with the vows. Jack, you will go first, followed by Emily. Then we will exchange rings, and I will pronounce you husband and wife. After that, you will walk out together, followed by Sue and Tyler. Simple, elegant, and filled with meaning."

They practiced once more, smoothing out any hesitations. Emily's heart swelled with love as she imagined the real moment the dress, the flowers, the music, and Jack's warm smile waiting at the altar.

"Perfect," Mayor Hutchison said, his voice full of satisfaction. "Now, let us head over to The Rusty Fork for dinner. I have reserved the back room for us, and dinners on me my wedding gift to you both."

They gathered their things, stepping out into the cool evening. The short drive to the restaurant was filled with light conversation and laughter. The Rusty Fork's private room was cozy, its wooden tables adorned with simple floral centerpieces and flickering candles. The warm glow of fairy lights draped across the ceiling created an inviting atmosphere.

As they settled into their seats, menus in hand, Debbie leaned closer to Emily. "You're glowing, sweetheart," she said warmly. "I can't wait to see you in your dress."

Emily's cheeks flushed with happiness. "Thanks, Mom. I am so excited and a little nervous."

Jack seated next to her, chuckled. "We all are. But it is going to be amazing."

The mayor smiled as drinks were served. "Now, let us relax and enjoy. Weddings are important, but family time like this is just as special. Let us thank the Lord for thus friendship and meal!"

As they ordered, the conversation turned to lighthearted stories. Sue recounted the time she and Emily had spent hours trying on dresses, while Tyler added a playful comment about his tuxedo finally arriving.

But it was Debbie who brought the table to life with a mischievous twinkle in her eye. "You know," she said, glancing between Emily and Jack, "it's funny how Jack told us all when he and Emily started dating that he couldn't cook to save his life."

Jack groaned, playfully covering his face. "Oh, here we go."

Debbie laughed. "And then, wouldn't you know it, on their first Thanksgiving together, this man woke up early and made a full English breakfast for Emily bacon, eggs, toast, the whole spread. It was delicious, she said. And since then, he has cooked up plenty of good meals. Guess someone was holding out on us!"

Emily giggled, nodding. "He really surprised me. And it turns out he is a fantastic cook when he wants to be."

Jack grinned sheepishly. "I just needed the right motivation. Emily brings out the best in me."

The table erupted in laughter and good-natured teasing.

Then Debbie, her eyes twinkling even more, leaned in and said, "Speaking of cooking disasters, let me tell you about our first Thanksgiving as a married couple."

Emily groaned, but everyone leaned in closer.

"I thought I was being so responsible," Debbie began, her tone light and full of humor. "I made sure the turkey was defrosting three days in advance on the countertop, of course. I went to work thinking I was ahead of schedule. When I got home... well, let us just say Lucy, our dog, had helped herself. There was turkey all over the kitchen floor, the living room carpet, even the hallway! She had dragged it everywhere. I nearly fainted!"

Randy chuckled, shaking his head. "I had to go to three different stores that night to find a turkey that was not frozen solid. And we barely made it through dinner without more mishaps."

Emily covered her mouth, laughing. "Oh, Lucy. I remember her!"

Debbie nodded, wiping her eyes. "That dog was a handful, but she made life interesting."

Sue giggled. "Sounds like you've always had a knack for turning chaos into a story, Debbie."

Debbie winked. "What can I say? It is a gift."

The conversation flowed easily, the laughter warm and the stories bringing everyone closer. Randy, though still showing traces of his reserved demeanor, finally joined in, sharing a few memories from Emily's childhood.

"She was always a good kid," he said, his voice gruff but affectionate. "Never needed much discipline. Made good grades, helped around the house. Well except for the milk incident."

Emily blushed. "Dad, not that story."

"Oh, yes," Randy insisted, his grin widening. "She used to spill her milk on the floor just so Lucy would come and lick it up. Did it every night until we finally put her in timeout. Thought it was the funniest thing ever."

Debbie laughed. "And there was that one time she came home from school with a note some boy had lice, and we had to wash her hair with that lice shampoo. She was so embarrassed, poor thing."

Emily covered her face with her hands, giggling. "I thought I was going to die from embarrassment."

But Randy's tone softened as he recalled a more meaningful lesson. "The most important one, though, was when she was throwing gravel across the road and hit a passing car. Scratched it good. I paid the guy $168 to fix it, and Emily had to do 168 extra chores one dollar per chore. Took her two and a half months, but she paid me back every cent."

Emily's voice was quiet but firm. "That taught me the value of money. I have never forgotten it."

Jack squeezed her hand, his eyes full of pride. "That is one of the things I admire most about you, Emily. You take responsibility and learn from your mistakes."

Randy gave a small nod. "Just treat her right, Jack. That is all I ask."

"I will, sir," Jack said sincerely.

As dessert was served, the mayor raised his glass. "To Emily and Jack," he said warmly. "May your love be steadfast, your home filled with laughter, and your journey blessed with friends and family."

The table echoed the toast with clinking glasses and murmurs of agreement. Emily's heart swelled with emotion, surrounded by love, laughter, and the promise of a new beginning.

The evening ended with hugs, reminders about wedding-day schedules, and a final round of stories. As they left The Rusty Fork and stepped into the cool night air, Emily felt Jack's arm slip around her waist.

"I'm ready," she whispered.

Jack kissed her temple. "Me too. Let us make this the start of forever."

They walked into the night, the glow of the restaurant's lights fading behind them and the future waiting just ahead.

# Chapter Fifteen: An Unexpected Reunion

The sun shone brightly over Pineville Community Church as the clock struck noon. The parking lot was already beginning to fill with cars, the air buzzing with the excitement of friends and family arriving for Emily and Jack's wedding.

Jack's truck rumbled into the lot, but his breath caught as he spotted something unexpected Chris Younger's tour bus, gleaming under the sunlight, parked casually near the fellowship hall.

"What in the world?" Jack murmured, pulling into a space. He killed the engine and stepped out, smoothing the front of his jacket. His heart raced, curiosity pulling him forward.

Inside the fellowship hall, the low hum of conversation and the scent of fresh flowers met him. As he stepped through the door, he caught sight of a familiar blonde figure Bethany, her easy grace and sparkling smile lighting up the room.

"Bethany!" Jack called out, his voice full of surprise and delight.

Bethany turned, her face breaking into a wide grin. "Jack!" She crossed the space between them, wrapping him in a warm hug. "You didn't think I'd miss this, did you?"

Jack laughed, stepping back to look her over. "What are you doing here? I thought you were tied up with studio work in Nashville."

Bethany winked. "I made time. Could not resist seeing you get married and give you a little surprise of my own."

Just then, a familiar, deep voice called from behind them. "Look who's talking about surprises!"

Jack turned to see Chris Younger, leaning casually against the fellowship hall's piano, his signature smile in place.

Jack's face lit up, and he crossed the room in a few quick strides. "Hey, you old dog! What are you doing here?"

Chris chuckled, stepping forward to pull Jack into a bear hug. "Old dog? You are the old dog around here, Jack."

They both laughed, the years of shared gigs and long nights on the road flashing between them. Jack's mind filled with memories of smoky bars, standing ovations, and after-hours breakfasts in Nashville diners.

"I can't believe you're here," Jack said, stepping back. "How long's it been since we shared a stage?"

Chris grinned. "Too long. I heard from Bethany you were getting married, and I figured, why not show up and see if you still remember how to carry a tune?"

Jack snorted. "Carry a tune? I have been carrying you for years, my friend."

They laughed again, the sound ringing through the hall. Then Chris's expression softened. "Bethany says you are coming back to Nashville part-time to record a Christmas album. What is this? Your too old to tour all year?"

Jack grinned, his eyes crinkling at the corners. "Not too old just slowing down to have a family. Emily's everything to me now. I figured it is time to balance the music with something even more important."

Chris clapped him on the back. "Good for you, man. It is about time. But I gotta ask what is the real story? You still got those pipes?"

Jack grinned mischievously. "As a matter of fact, ... I was hoping to ask you a favor."

Chris raised an eyebrow. "Anything. You know that."

Jack glanced at Bethany. "Do you have the flash drive of that new song?"

Bethany's eyes sparkled as she reached into her bag and produced a sleek black drive. "Right here."

Jack grinned, taking it from her and moving toward the small sound system set up in the corner. "Let us play it a couple of times. I want to sing it tonight right after the bride's dance. It is called It's

Christmas Time in the City. I will lead the vocals, and I would love for you to play with me."

Chris's eyes widened. "A Christmas song? At your wedding?"

Jack nodded. "For the people. For Pineville. And for Emily. Plus, I want to have Tyler sing it with me. He is coming to Nashville after he graduates, and this will be his first chance to step into the spotlight."

Chris's grin widened. "Now that is a plan. Let us hear it."

They gathered around as Jack loaded the song onto the system. The first notes filled the hall a gentle guitar melody over soft piano chords, with lyrics that painted scenes of holiday streets, the magic of small towns, and the warmth of family.

The first play through was met with nods and murmurs of approval. On the second run, Chris joined in with harmonies, while Jack confidently took the lead. By the time the song faded, they were both grinning.

Bethany clapped her hands. "It is perfect. Jack, you sound better than ever. And Tyler will shine beside you."

Jack's heart swelled with pride and anticipation. He imagined the look on Emily's face when the surprise unfolded, the joy of sharing his music with friends, family, and his new bride.

Chris slung his arm around Jack's shoulders. "You are full of surprises today. Let us make this wedding one Pineville will not forget."

Jack nodded, his heart light. "Agreed. Now, let us get ready. It is showtime."

As they finished rehearsing the song and prepared to take their places, Jack could not help but marvel at how life had come full circle. From those early gigs in Nashville to this moment surrounded by friends, love, and the promise of new beginnings.

He was ready.

Jack glanced at his watch, the second hand ticking ever closer to 1:00 p.m. "Three minutes," he muttered to himself, feeling a rush of nervous energy course through him.

Chris Younger gave him a playful nudge. "You'd better move it, old man. Do not want to miss your own wedding."

# Chapter Sixteen: Wedding and Reception

Jack laughed, nodding. "You are right. I must get to my spot."

He hurried through the side door of the church, his heart pounding as he imagined Emily's radiant smile. But as he stepped into the corridor behind the sanctuary, he stopped short. There, standing tall and looking healthier than he had in weeks, was Pastor Raymin.

"Pastor!" Jack exclaimed, his voice filled with surprise and joy.

Pastor Raymin grinned, a touch of pink returning to his cheeks. "I am feeling much better, Jack. The doctors cleared me this morning, and I would not miss this for the world. Mayor Hutchison graciously stepped aside when he heard I was well enough to officiate."

Jack's heart swelled. "Emily is going to be so surprised. She will be over the moon."

"I hope so," Pastor Raymin said warmly. "Let's give her a wedding day she'll never forget."

As the minutes ticked down, Jack made his way toward the front of the church, catching sight of Tyler, who stood waiting with a grin.

"Ready for this, Tyler?" Jack asked, clapping his friend on the back.

Tyler nodded, his eyes sparkling. "Absolutely. Let us make this perfect."

The low hum of conversation in the sanctuary quieted as the music began to play. Pastor Raymin stepped to the podium, his presence commanding attention. The entire church erupted in spontaneous applause, their joy spilling over into exclamations of "Hallelujah!" and "Praise God!"

Jack glanced back toward the entrance just as the doors opened and Emily, radiant in her gown, stepped into view on her father Randy's arm. For a moment, time seemed to stand still. Emily's eyes widened as she saw Pastor Raymin standing at the podium, and tears welled up, threatening to spill over.

Randy whispered softly, "He made it."

Emily nodded, her voice catching. "He did."

As they walked slowly down the aisle, the soft strains of the processional music filled the air, weaving through the sanctuary like a blessing. The sunlight filtering through the stained-glass windows bathed the space in warm hues of gold and rose.

Jack's breath caught in his throat as he watched Emily draw closer. Her eyes shimmered with emotion, and her lips curved into a tender smile that was just for him.

When they reached the front, Pastor Raymin greeted them both with a smile full of love and pride. "Who gives this woman to be married to this man?" he asked.

Randy's voice was strong and steady. "Her mother and I do."

He stepped aside, placing Emily's hand in Jack's. Jack squeezed her hand gently, feeling the depth of her love and the quiet promise of forever.

The ceremony proceeded without a hitch. Pastor Raymin's voice rang clear as he guided them through their vows, the congregation hanging on every word. Emily and Jack's voices trembled with emotion but held steady as they pledged their love and commitment before family, friends, and God.

When it came time to exchange rings, Jack slipped Emily's band onto her finger, his hands steady despite the rush of feelings surging through him. Emily's fingers trembled only slightly as she placed Jack's ring on his hand.

Pastor Raymin's eyes glistened as he raised his hands. "By the authority vested in me and in the presence of God and this gathering, I pronounce you husband and wife. You may kiss the bride."

Cheers and applause erupted from the congregation as Jack pulled Emily into his arms and pressed a tender kiss to her lips. They lingered there for a moment, lost in each other, as the joy of the day washed over them.

Hand in hand, they turned to face the congregation, their smiles radiant. The church filled with clapping, laughter, and joyful exclamations. As they walked back down the aisle together, Jack caught sight of Chris and Bethany, both grinning and giving him a thumbs-up.

Tyler and Sue followed behind them, their steps light and filled with happiness. Debbie dabbed her eyes with a tissue, leaning into Randy's side as he wiped away his own quiet tears.

Outside, the sun shone down on the steps of the church, and as the newlyweds appeared into the light, the air was filled with cheers and the gentle ringing of church bells.

Jack turned to Emily, his voice low and full of emotion. "You were right it was perfect."

Emily's eyes sparkled as she leaned into him. "We were surrounded by love. That is all we needed."

They stood together on the church steps, the applause still echoing around them, ready to step into a lifetime of shared memories and love.

Sandra had the church party and pastor go back inside for pictures before going to the reception.

Inside the church, the air buzzed with quiet laughter and whispered congratulations. Emily stood near the altar, her peach-tinted lace gown shimmering under the gentle glow of the stained-glass windows. Jack adjusted his bow tie with a self-conscious smile, his eyes never leaving Emily's. Pastor Raymin gathered the family and wedding party around, instructing them to pose in various groupings for the photographer.

"Sandra, you and Pastor stand to the side," he said with a gentle hand on her shoulder. "I want the immediate family first."

Sandra nodded, her eyes misting with emotion as she guided the others into place. Flashbulbs lit up the church like tiny stars, capturing moments that would become cherished memories.

After the family photos were done, Pastor Raymin motioned for the entire church party the Sue, Tyler, and the couple to gather near the altar for a grand photo. Emily's friends adjusted their dresses, and Tyler shared lighthearted jabs, but when the camera clicked, everyone wore their most radiant smiles.

"All right," Pastor Raymin said, stepping back, "that is perfect. Now let us get a few shots of just the two of you."

As the wedding party stepped aside, Jack and Emily stood together at the altar, his hand resting gently at her waist, her fingers laced through his. The photographer captured the tenderness of the moment the way Jack gazed at Emily as though she were the most beautiful woman in the world, the way Emily's smile brightened in his presence.

Pastor Raymin leaned toward them with a warm smile. "Let's take one more, and then it's off to celebrate."

With that, Jack kissed Emily's forehead, the camera catching the sweet intimacy just before the two turned toward the church doors.

"Ready for the reception?" Jack whispered.

Emily nodded, her cheeks flushed. "I'm ready if you are."

Hand in hand, they walked down the aisle once more this time not as a bride and groom leaving the altar but as husband and wife stepping into a new life together.

The fellowship hall of Pineville Community Church shimmered with the soft glow of fairy lights strung from wall to wall. Tables were dressed in crisp white linens, bouquets of peach and white roses, and flickering candles. The laughter of guests mingled with the gentle clink of glasses as everyone gathered to celebrate Jack and Emily's new beginning.

As Emily stepped through the doorway into the hall, she paused, her heart catching at the sight of so many familiar faces. Bethany approached her with a radiant smile.

The entire group of guests stood and clapped welcoming the newlyweds.

"Emily," Bethany greeted warmly, pulling her into a light embrace. "You look absolutely stunning."

Emily returned the smile, her voice bubbling with happiness. "Thank you, Bethany. And I have to say, Jack is doing much better this time seeing you here. No awkward run-ins like last time!" Both women chuckled softly, the tension from the past now gone amid the joy of the evening.

They exchanged a few more words of congratulations and mutual respect before making their way to their tables. The delicious aroma of the catered meal filled the air as servers bustled about, preparing for dinner.

Just as everyone was settling into their seats, Tyler stood up, a nervous but determined look on his face. He cleared his throat, drawing the room's attention. He used a spoon and clanged it against the glass of champagne.

"I, uh... I am not great with speeches," Tyler began, his voice cracking slightly. "But I could not let today go by without saying something. Five months ago, you all knew me as the town menace. Me and my gang we would tear up property, cause chaos. We thought we were tough guys, but we were just lost."

His voice steadied, his eye's finding Jack.

"It was Jack here who turned me around. The second time I met him, I was ready to well, to beat the living you-know-what out of him. But he stopped me. Taught me, right then and there, that I knew nothing about fighting about real strength."

The room was silent, the guests leaning in to listen.

"He came to the jail, made me read a note, and that day, he became like a dad to me," Tyler said, his voice thick with emotion. "He took me in, showed me what it meant to be a man, a Christian, and to respect people. And he taught me how to defend myself not with fists, but with heart."

He raised his glass. "A toast to my second dad, Jack, and his beautiful wife, Emily."

The guests erupted in applause, their glasses raised high. Jack stood, his voice low as he embraced Tyler. "I'm proud of you, son."

The applause had not yet faded when Sue rose from her seat, her cheeks pink with emotion.

"I've worked for Emily for four years," Sue said, her voice clear. "Started as a part-time worker during school, and now I am her assistant manager. But more than that we are not just coworkers. We are best friends. She is like a second mom to me, always encouraging me, always supporting me. And I could not be happier to be here today to celebrate her wedding."

She raised her glass, smiling through glistening eyes. "Cheers to Emily and Jack!"

"Cheers!" echoed around the room, a chorus of love and celebration.

Pastor Raymin, radiant with happiness, stepped forward to offer grace. His prayer, warm and full of gratitude, blessed not only the meal but the community gathered to celebrate this day of love and new beginnings.

"Let us bow our heads," Pastor Raymin began, his voice steady and full of love.

"Heavenly Father,

We come before You with grateful hearts,

Thankful for this day of joy and the union of Jack and Emily.

Thank You for bringing them together in love and faith,

And for the family and friends gathered to celebrate their new beginning.

Lord, we ask Your blessing upon this meal we are about to share,

That it may nourish our bodies and remind us of Your provision.

Bless the hands that prepared it,

And may this time of fellowship strengthen the bonds between us all.

We especially lift Jack and Emily before You today.

Bless their marriage with patience, understanding, and unwavering love.

Guide them as they walk this journey of life together,

And fill their home with peace, laughter, and the light of Your presence.

May they always look to You as their source of strength,

And may their love for each other reflect Your love for us all.

In Jesus' holy name, we pray.

Amen."

After grace, the meal commenced plates filled with delicious food, laughter spilling across tables as stories and memories were shared.

As the last plates were cleared and the air filled with the hum of conversation and clinking glasses, the lights dimmed slightly. A familiar figure stepped onto the small stage at the front of the hall Chris Younger, dressed sharply, his signature grin lighting up the room.

The guests erupted into applause, cheers, and whistles as Chris raised his microphone.

"Wow, Pineville, you know how to make a guy feel welcome," he said, his voice warm and easy. "I have known Jack for ten years now. We have done gigs together, shared stories, and when Bethany asked me if I had come out for his wedding, I did not give it a second thought. I knew I had to be here."

The crowd clapped louder, excitement rising.

Chris's gaze softened as it found Emily and Jack. "Now, it is time for the bride's dance. And I have picked a special song for you two one that is all about love, commitment, and finding that one person who makes everything worthwhile."

He strummed the opening chords of his hit "You," the romantic melody filling the hall. As the song swept through the room, Jack stood and extended his hand to Emily, guiding her onto the dance floor. Under the soft glow of the lights, they danced lost in the music and each other, swaying in perfect harmony.

When the song ended, the applause was thunderous. Chris stepped back to the microphone, a playful smile lighting his face.

"Before we continue," he said, "I want to invite a couple of special people to join me on stage Jack and Tyler. Come on up here, guys."

Tyler's eyes widened in surprise, but Jack gave him an encouraging nudge. "Come on, buddy. Let's do this."

They joined Chris on stage. Chris grinned as he turned to his band.

"These guys have been practicing something special," Chris said. "My band's learned the music, and we are ready to back them up. Jack and Tyler are going to perform It's Christmas Time in the City a song Jack wrote with Pineville in mind. Let us make some magic."

Chris's band, already tuned and ready, struck up the opening chords. The warm, inviting melody filled the room, rich with guitar and keys. Jack took the lead on vocals, his voice strong and steady, while Tyler joined in on harmonies, his youthful energy blending seamlessly. The music, backed by Chris's talented band, created a full, vibrant sound that wrapped around the audience like a hug.

The crowd swayed, clapped, and cheered, many standing to join in. Some wiped away tears; others stood with arms around each other, moved by the heartfelt lyrics and the unity of the performance.

As the final note echoed through the hall, a moment of silence hung in the air then the room erupted into applause, cheers, and calls for an encore. Jack and Tyler stood side by side, beaming with pride. Chris gave them each a playful pat on the back.

"That was incredible," Chris said into the mic, his voice echoing the room's excitement. "Jack, Tyler you are something special. And Pineville you have gotten yourselves a pair of stars to be proud of."

The reception continued long into the evening, filled with dancing, laughter, and the deep bonds of family and community. For Jack and

Emily, it was a perfect ending to a perfect day a celebration of love, friendship, and the promise of a lifetime together.

Chris addressed the audience, "we are going to take a small break while Emily and Jack do some traditional wedding events.

Amid the joyful chatter, Sandra clapped her hands for attention. "All right, everyone, clear a space in the center! It is time for a little fun!"

With eager smiles, guests pushed chairs aside and created a circle in the middle of the hall. Jack stood, grinning mischievously, and took Emily's hand, leading her to a chair in the center of the room. She laughed, her cheeks flushed with excitement, as she settled onto the chair, smoothing her peach-tinted lace skirt over her knees.

Jack turned to Tyler and whispered something. Moments later, Tyler handed Jack a pair of blindfolds. The crowd erupted in laughter and whistles.

"Oh no, you are not! Were married now!" Emily teased, her eyes sparkling with both amusement and mock protest.

Jack grinned wider. "Oh yes, I am," he said, looping the blindfolds around his head dramatically and pretending to fumble as though he could not see. The room roared with laughter.

"I'm going in blind!" he declared, dropping to one knee. With exaggerated caution, he reached beneath Emily's dress, his hand brushing along the layers of lace and tulle. The guests were howling with laughter as he dramatically pretended to search.

"Jack Whitaker, don't you dare take too long!" Emily laughed breathlessly, her face turning a brilliant shade of pink.

Finally, with a triumphant flourish, Jack pulled the delicate garter free and held it high above his head like a trophy. The crowd erupted in applause and cheers.

He stood and turned toward all the single men, calling out, "All right, fellas who's ready to catch this?" Pastor Raymin made his way into the group. "Pastor this is for single men only" Jack yelled. The crowd laughed.

The men crowded forward, playfully jostling for position. Jack gave the garter a good spin and launched it into the air. It flew in a graceful arc and landed squarely in the hands of Tyler who caught it with mock pride and bowed dramatically to the laughing crowd.

Jack, still grinning from ear to ear, turned back to Emily and pulled her to her feet. He leaned close and whispered, "Your turn, Mrs. Whitaker."

Emily, her laughter still bubbling, was handed the bridal bouquet. She turned to face the eager group of single women standing to one side, all pretending to nonchalantly adjust their hair or fix their dresses.

"On the count of three," Emily called. "One... two... three!"

She tossed the bouquet over her shoulder, and it sailed perfectly into the hands of a blushing Sue. The women cheered, and Sue the lucky catcher raised the flowers in triumph.

Emily yelled, "look out Tyler, Sue caught the flowers you know what that means?" Both Sue and Tylers face blushed.

The crowd roared in laughter!

The crowd was still buzzing with laughter from the bouquet and garter antics when Sandra called out, "All right everyone, it's time for the cake cutting!"

Servers wheeled in a towering, three-tiered cake adorned with delicate peach-colored roses and tiny white sugar pearls. Jack and Emily stood side by side, holding the silver knife together, their hands layered as they prepared to make the ceremonial first cut.

"Don't be shy now!" one guest called, prompting cheers and teasing laughter.

Jack grinned. "You ready, Em?"

"Let's do it," she said with a playful smirk.

They sliced into the cake, lifting out a piece with careful precision. But before they could politely feed each other, Jack mischievously dabbed a bit of frosting onto Emily's nose. The crowd gasped and burst into laughter.

"Oh, you're asking for it now!" Emily declared, laughing as she scooped a small dollop of frosting and smeared it across Jack's cheek.

The crowd roared with approval. Jack retaliated by pressing a bit of cake against Emily's lips, and she responded by wiping frosting onto his forehead.

They both laughed uncontrollably, frosting and crumbs decorating their faces like children at play. The guests clapped and cheered, phones flashing to capture the hilarious moment.

Pastor Raymin chuckled, shaking his head with a smile. "That's what love looks like, folks!" he called out.

After a quick wipe with napkins and some good-natured ribbing from family and friends Jack and Emily shared a sweet, frosting-kissed kiss.

Just then, the band shifted into a smooth transition. Chris Young, standing with his guitar at the ready, gave the couple a grin. "All right, Jack and Emily," he said into the mic, "now that we've had cake, how about a little music to dance it off?"

The band launched into a lively tune, filling the fellowship hall with rich country melodies. Jack reached for Emily's hand, pulling her onto the dance floor. Their second dance as husband and wife was a perfect blend of tenderness and joy, their movements graceful and lighthearted beneath the warm glow of the string lights.

As they danced, Chris sang with his signature smooth, heartfelt vocals, his band keeping the rhythm tight and inviting. Couples joined in, filling the floor with swirling dresses and tapping boots, the music carrying everyone's spirits higher.

When the song ended, Chris grinned from the stage. "Congratulations, Jack, and Emily! Wishing you a lifetime of love and a little more cake in the future!"

The crowd cheered, and the music rolled on. Chris and his band kept the atmosphere lively, their setlist blending slow love songs with foot-stomping country hits, perfectly matching the joyful energy of the evening.

# Chapter Seventeen: Final Surprises and New Beginnings

The fellowship hall's glow softened as the evening waned, but the spirit of celebration only deepened. The tables, now slightly scattered with empty plates and drained glasses, were surrounded by guests engaged in soft conversations and warm laughter. Chris Younger's surprise performance still echoed in everyone's minds, and the town of Pineville buzzed with pride at having such a memorable evening.

Emily and Jack found a quiet moment together near the edge of the dance floor, their hands still entwined. "I don't want this night to end," Emily whispered, her head resting against Jack's shoulder.

Jack kissed the top of her head. "Neither do I. But it is only the beginning, sweetheart. We have a lifetime of moments just like this ahead of us."

Just then, Tyler approached, a shy but excited smile lighting his face. "Jack, Emily Bethany just pulled me aside. She said Chris wants to talk to me."

Emily's eyebrows lifted. "Really? About what?"

Tyler shrugged, his cheeks flushing with anticipation. "I am not sure. But it is something big."

Before Jack could respond, Bethany herself appeared, her polished appearance only slightly softened by the warmth of the evening. "There you are, Tyler. Chris wants to chat with you about Nashville. He is impressed with your performance tonight. Said you have the voice and presence to make it big."

Tyler's eyes widened. "Are you serious?"

Bethany nodded. "Very. He wants you to come down and meet his producer. You will need to finish school, of course, but Chris is offering to mentor you when you are ready."

Jack clapped a hand on Tyler's shoulder. "That is amazing, son. This is your chance to chase your dream just like I did years ago. And now, you will have a head start."

Emily grinned, her eyes shimmering with pride. "We are so proud of you, Tyler. And do not worry you will always have Pineville to come home to."

As Tyler left with Bethany to meet Chrises producer backstage, Emily and Jack returned to the dance floor. The band struck up a gentle tune, and they swayed together, lost in the rhythm and the shared memories of the day.

Sue approached with Mary by her side, both women beaming. "Emily, Jack," Sue said, her voice light with joy, "Mary and I just wanted to say congratulations again. And I wanted you to know after tonight, we will keep the music store running smoothly while you are away on your honeymoon and Nashville. Everything is in good hands."

Mary nodded, her face alight with determination. "It's the least we can do after everything you've done for us."

Emily hugged them both. "Thank you. I cannot tell you how much that means to us."

The evening rolled on with laughter, more dancing, and a final toast led by Pastor Raymin, his voice resonant and filled with gratitude. "To Jack and Emily," he said, lifting his glass high. "May your love shine brighter with each passing day, and may your journey together be blessed with faith, joy, and community."

The entire hall echoed with a chorus of "Hear, hear!" as glasses clinked and the warmth of the evening filled every heart.

As the reception ended, Jack found himself once again standing by Chris, both men watching the crowd dissipate. "Thanks for everything, Chris," Jack said, his voice thick with emotion. "You being here it made this day even more special."

Chris grinned. "Anything for an old friend. And do not be a stranger, Jack. Nashville's always there when you are ready to record that Christmas album."

Jack laughed softly. "I'll hold you to that."

Outside, as the cool night air wrapped around them, Emily and Jack stood beneath the soft glow of the streetlights. The stars sparkled above Pineville, and the last strains of music from the hall drifted into the night.

Emily leaned into Jack, her voice a whisper. "This really was the perfect day."

Jack kissed her gently, his arms tightening around her. "And it is only the beginning. Our best days are still ahead."

As they walked toward their car, hand in hand, the lights of Pineville glowing behind them, it was clear that while one chapter had ended, a new and brighter one was just beginning.

Jack helped Emily in the passenger side, Jack got in the driver's side. As the car pulled toward the street, they could hear the clinging of tin cans hitting the pavement. They both laughed.

But Jack turned right and not left?

Emily looked at Jack, "What are you up to?"

Jack grinned, "my gift to my bride I booked a room in the Poconos it is just an hour up the road. For our short honeymoon."

Emily, "I do not have any clothes? "

Jack turned his head looking at Emily, "yes you do, I had Sue pack you a bag and put it in the trunk on Friday. Remember she left the store to go eat lunch, that is when she did it!"

# Chapter 18: The Pocono Honeymoon

Jack and Emily arrived at their honeymoon suite in the Poconos just as the late evening sun dipped behind the rolling hills. The hotel staff had outdone themselves. A chilled bottle of champagne, adorned with a ribbon, waited on the side table as a welcome gift. A fire crackled in the stone fireplace, its glow casting a golden hue over the room.

Emily's eyes widened in delight. "Oh, Jack, look at this! It is beautiful."

Jack chuckled as he closed the door behind them. "Not as beautiful as you," he said, wrapping his arms around her waist and planting a gentle kiss on her temple.

The suite was everything they had hoped for and more. A heart-shaped Jacuzzi tub sat beneath a wide mirror, waiting to be filled with warm, bubbling water. A plush king-size bed with a mountain of pillows beckoned them to relax. Rose petals were sprinkled across the bedspread a surprise touch from the hotel that made Emily's cheeks flush with happiness.

Jack opened the champagne and poured two glasses. As they toasted quietly to their new life Jack's glass clinking softly against Emily's they savored the moment of just being together, without the busyness of the wedding day.

Soon, Emily turned toward the bubbling Jacuzzi with a smile. "I think that tub is calling our name," she said playfully.

Jack grinned, setting down his glass. "I couldn't agree more."

With a soft laugh, Emily slowly slipped out of her dress, her fingers trembling slightly from excitement and shyness. Jack stood still for a moment, his eyes drinking her in seeing her for the first time.

"You're absolutely stunning," he whispered, his voice filled with admiration.

Emily's cheeks flushed deeper, her heart fluttering at the sincerity in his gaze. She stepped closer to him and placed a hand on his chest.

"You're not so bad yourself, Mr. Whitaker," she teased. "In fact, you're quite handsome."

Jack laughed, the sound deep and warm. He began to undress as well, and Emily watched with a mixture of tenderness and anticipation. As his shirt fell to the floor and his slacks followed, she traced her gaze over him, her lips curving into a soft smile.

"You're perfect," she murmured, stepping close to press a kiss to his chest.

Their shared laughter and mutual compliments filled the room, weaving a moment of intimacy that felt both playful and profound.

Together, they slipped into the warm, bubbling water of the heart-shaped Jacuzzi, the heat enveloping them as they relaxed against each other. Jack's arm slid around Emily's shoulders, pulling her close.

For the first time, they were completely alone, just the two of them no guests, no cameras, no distractions. They shared stories about the wedding day, laughing over the garter toss, the cake smearing, and the joy of dancing together with Chris Younger's band filling the air.

Later, as the water cooled and the fire crackled lower, they wrapped themselves in thick towels and settled by the fireplace, savoring the last sips of champagne. Jack's voice was soft. "I am glad we did this. Even if it is just a weekend, it is ours."

Emily leaned against his chest, her voice a whisper. "And we'll plan a longer honeymoon after the album."

They made a promise right then, surrounded by the glow of the fire and the fading light from the window that this was just the beginning of many more adventures to come.

As the flames danced lower and the night deepened, Jack took Emily's hand and gently led her from the fireside to the king-sized bed. With a shared glance, they slipped beneath the covers, their hearts beating in harmony. There, in the quiet warmth of the honeymoon suite, they finally shed the last of their shyness and embraced each other fully.

For the first time, they reveled in the intimacy of being husband and wife, the thrill of discovering each other's touch, and the tender beauty of lovemaking born not from lust but from deep affection and commitment. Their laughter mingled with soft whispers and passionate kisses, their love unfolding naturally in the privacy of the night.

As they drifted into sleep, wrapped in each other's arms, the promise of forever felt closer than ever.

The morning sun filtered softly through the lace curtains of their honeymoon suite in the Poconos, casting a gentle glow over the room. The scent of fresh coffee and warm pastries wafted in as hotel staff quietly delivered a sumptuous breakfast in bed. Jack and Emily, still wrapped in the warmth of their love, sat up to find a tray adorned with golden croissants, fresh fruit, scrambled eggs, and two flutes of sparkling cider.

"Good morning, Mrs. Whitaker," Jack said, his eyes twinkling as he handed Emily a cup of coffee.

Emily smiled, her heart full. "Good morning, Mr. Whitaker."

They savored their meal, feeding each other bites and sharing laughter over memories from their wedding day. The intimacy of the moment, the realization that they were now husband and wife, enveloped them in a cocoon of joy.

After breakfast, they moved to the plush couch by the fireplace. Jack stoked the fire, and soon, flames danced, casting a warm glow around the room. They nestled together, Emily's head resting on Jack's shoulder, his arm wrapped around her.

"This feels like a dream," Emily whispered.

Jack kissed her forehead. "It's our reality now."

They spent the afternoon in each other's arms, talking about their future, their hopes, and the adventures that awaited them. The comfort of their connection, the shared dreams, and the love that bound them made the hours slip by unnoticed.

As the sun began to set, casting golden hues across the sky, they knew their time in the Poconos was ending. They had to return home that evening to prepare for their early morning flight to Nashville, where they would begin recording their Christmas album.

"I wish we had more time here," Emily said, her voice tinged with longing.

Jack took her hands in his. "We will. Let us promise each other a longer honeymoon in the future. After the album is done."

Emily nodded, a smile spreading across her face. "It's a promise."

They packed their bags, taking one last look around the suite that had been their haven. As they stepped out, hand in hand, the cool evening air greeted them, a reminder of the journey ahead.

Driving home, they reflected on their whirlwind of a wedding, the joy of their brief honeymoon, and the exciting path that lay before them. Their love, solidified in vows and shared moments, was the foundation upon which they would build their future.

As they pulled into their driveway, Jack turned to Emily. "Here's to forever."

Emily leaned in, her eyes shining. "Forever starts now."

Jack says, "and Nashville starts tomorrow!"